Cady and the
Bear Necklace

To Teagan –
I hope you
enjoy this!
An Dallan
AgD. 2019

Cady and the Bear Necklace

Ann Dallman

Three Towers Press

Milwaukee, Wisconsin

Published by
Three Towers Press
An imprint of HenschelHAUS Publishing, Inc.
www.henschelHAUSbooks.com

ISBN: 978159598-685-6
E-ISBN: 978159598-686-3
LCCN: 2018964370

Interior layout: WaterStreet Creative
Cover design by Haley Greenfeather English

Printed in the United States of America

DEDICATION:

~~~~~~~~~~~~~~

This book is a "thank you" to my students—they know who they are.
May all their dreams come true.

Table of Contents

Chapter 1
Watch Out!

ran fast that night on my way to meet John Ray Chicaug in the woods. But I ran fast for another reason too. I wanted to forget about the eagle feather.

I'd snuck out of the house after my dad fell asleep in front of the television. I waited until his rumbling snores were louder than the news program he'd been watching. I'd crept from my bedroom into the upstairs hallway and down the back staircase into the kitchen. I turned off the security system Dad had installed the day after we'd moved into this old house on the south side of town. He's a real security freak so it's a good thing he's handy with electronics. I carefully opened the outside door and then started running.

It wasn't late, only about 7:30 or so, but because it's early spring the nights can get cold. Not winter cold but cold enough to chill your bones if you don't keep moving.

My name is Cady Whirlwind Thunder and nothing was going to keep me from meeting John Ray. John Ray is the best-looking guy at my new school. Until he asked me to meet him in the woods, I thought I was invisible to him because I'm the new girl. I'm almost 14 years old and John Ray is 16. I'm in love with him.

Last week I told Irish Morrissey, my best friend, that I love John Ray and she told me to knock it off. I've only been at Four Eagles School for three months and I'm happy to even have a friend. The school is on a Woodland Indian reservation about twenty miles from Barnesville in the Upper Peninsula of Michigan. Sault Sainte Marie, Canada, is less than two hundred miles from here, which tells you how far north we are.

I'm an enrolled member of the Woodland Nation but my school is open to everyone, natives and non-natives, and has 184 students from kindergarten through high school. I know this because I asked Irish and she knows everything, at least that's what she tells me.

"Don't you think you're getting carried away about someone who doesn't even know you exist?" Irish asked me when I told her how I felt about John Ray.

"Yeah, probably, but so what?" When I thought about John Ray I didn't even know who I was anymore. I daydreamed about his hand brushing against my arm and then I'd hold my breath and wonder if he'd bend down to kiss me because he's taller than I am.

I smiled as if I could hear Irish say, "*Ney*," and then she'd laugh and shake her head. In our words, in Indian talk, "*Ney*" means "Silly girl, probably won't happen."

That magical night, the night I went running, I wore my black jeans, a navy hoodie, and my almost worn-out running shoes. They used to be bright blue and silver and even though they're faded, they were still my favorites and I'd hoped they'd bring me good luck. I'd pulled my hood up to cover my hair because running was easier when it wasn't blowing in my face. My hair was brown until two weeks ago, when I dyed it black— and now it looked dense and heavy. I stuck my skull-and-cross-bones earrings, carved out of something that looks like white chalk, into my earlobes. I felt older when I wore them even though each one is only about the size of a dime. I tried not to wear them around my dad because he doesn't like anything that he thinks is "sinister" (his word, not mine), but I figured they were so small that he probably wouldn't notice them. I'd been in enough trouble with him during the past two years and we are just starting to get along again. I have a wicked temper and a short fuse. I know that's not good, but it's hard to change once your reputation is set.

That night I went running to the woods, my heart thumped and thumped. It was so loud that I'd crossed my fingers and pleaded with the universe not to let it explode through my chest. What if John Ray heard it? I swear I would have died of embarrassment.

The gym teacher at my last school taught us that when we're excited we should take deep breaths through our noses and then breathe out slowly through our mouths. I tried it a few times and it helped to calm my thoughts.

Maybe something good will finally happen for me. Maybe things will change now that we've moved.

My heart quieted down but I could still hear the soft thwack, thwack my shoes made as they hit the ground. It was spring so the leaves on the trees along my route rustled as the wind blew them in swirls around me. A blue jay squawked a harsh *jaay-jaay* until a dog barked, making me pick up my pace.

I slowed down so that I could pull my beat-up silver cell phone from the pocket of my jeans to check the time. Fifteen minutes had passed since I left my house. I looked up from my phone and spotted the rusted yellow trash can that marked the start of the trail to our meeting place.

I didn't know why John Ray wanted to meet me. I crossed my fingers and hoped he would try to hug me because I wanted to let him hold me extra long before I pulled away. Just thinking about that sent shivers through me. Or would he want to tell me a story? That's not as lame as it sounds. We both go to school on the reservation even though I live in town and John Ray lives on the rez with his family. His family is known for their storytelling.

"That family's got good medicine. They tell good stories," I'd heard one old lady tell another at a potluck dinner last month at the rez's community center.

"Yeah," another old lady said, laughing. "You've got to watch out for those smooth talkers, those storytellers. They can sweet-talk a person into doing almost anything."

Those four old ladies laughed so hard they were crying. Actually, it sounded more like cackling, but it was a happy sound. Because I'm new here I didn't know what to think. For a moment I even wondered if that was a warning because I'd been taught that stories are used to teach lessons and to pass on our culture. They're not just for entertainment but these ladies were laughing as if stories were just for fun. Actually, they made it even sound kind of nasty and I didn't like that. For Pete's sake, they're old. I mean really old, like my grandma's age.

I hoped John Ray wouldn't want to party. When kids meet up at night, they like to drink beer or anything else they can get from the older kids and smoke cigarettes or other stuff. I tasted beer once but spit it out because it tasted like dirty socks. Between you and me, I'd rather drink ginger ale, especially the kind they make in Michigan, and listen to John Ray tell a story.

I picked up my pace and then slowed down to follow a curve in the trail until I spotted him waiting for me next to some pine trees lined up in rows on either side of the path. I pulled my hood down so John Ray could see my hair. He wore jeans, scuffed brown leather ankle boots, and his black letter jacket with red sleeves and white lettering. I'd know that jacket anywhere because I've watched him so often at school. His name was stitched on the front and the name of our school, Four Eagles School, was underneath that.

We'd moved here from Minnesota where I would have attended a regular high school with grades 9 through 12. Four Eagles is different because it has a kindergarten, an elementary school and a high school. The hallways and floors are decorated with designs of long, stretched-out arrows in yellow and white and black and red. Four hallways branch off from the main entrance. Each hallway has its own color of arrow running down the center.

The night I went running was one of those magical nights when you could almost see the shadows on the moon. I crossed my fingers and made a wish that John Ray liked me as much as I liked him.

"*Ahau*, Cady," he murmured as he reached out to touch my shoulder. "So you came after all." I loved it that I could look up at him. I'm 5 feet 8 inches and John Ray is four inches taller than me. The softness in his voice stopped me more than his touch. I nodded my head then raised it and looked back at him.

"Follow me," he instructed.

He signaled for me to keep up. It was almost 8 o'clock. Darkness deepened as we went into the woods and I was glad I'd brought a flashlight. It was about 10 inches long and the light it threw was hard and bright. John Ray carried his own flashlight and we needed both of them to light our way through the heavy shadows cast by the trees surrounding us. The stars disappeared because of the blanket of dark green leaves above us. The trees reached higher than the highest buildings in Minneapolis. At least that's how it seemed to me that night.

Probably pine, birch, sugar maple and cedar. Oak? No, not this close to the beach. Here I go daydreaming again. Quit being such a dork, Cady, and concentrate on following John Ray.

I blinked my eyes and walked faster. A few minutes later I heard the soft and rhythmic sound of the waves washing onto the beach.

Although it was dark, it seemed safer outdoors than it did at home where the television always blared. My dad and his new wife, Francine, yell at each other a lot and that wakes up my baby brother, Colson. Then he starts crying. Dad met Francine two years ago at a powwow in Barnesville, her home town, and that's why we'd moved here after the baby was born.

I laughed out loud, which was embarrassing because it sounded more like a snort. That always happened when I was nervous.

"What's so funny, Cady?"

"Nothing. But these trees make me think about my dad. He's old like these trees, he's almost 55 and Francine, my stepmonster, is only 24. So now it's different at home from when it was only my dad and me. I had to sneak out to meet you because I don't think he trusts me since we moved here."

And there was more. Like how it didn't seem like I really had a home anymore. Like how I was starting to feel like I was in the way. Like how I wondered if my dad even loved me because he sure didn't treat me like he used to when it was only the two of us.

It made me so frustrated that sometimes I'd stuff myself with chips and popcorn or candy bars and red licorice just to stop the loneliness and not to think about what had happened before we'd moved here. It hadn't been my fault. But maybe it was one more reason for the move.

John Ray stopped and looked at me.

"My coach would tell you to suck it up."

"Well, maybe your coach should try living with us. I could sneak out tonight because the baby has an ear infection and cried all day before finally falling asleep. Then Dad and Francine fell asleep. I guess they were too tired to know if I was even home or not."

There, I'd said it. I'd spilled my guts to the best-looking guy on the rez while we were running through the woods. And because he was leading the way, I was able to really look at John Ray. His heavy, dark brown hair was cut in a blunt, straight line

6

and touched his shoulders. He's quick on his feet and filled with so much energy that the air around him vibrates.

I pushed those thoughts away and hurried to keep up with him. A few minutes later, I could smell a campfire. It didn't smell like the fires my dad or older brother built. They used aged wood, which burned dry and made a crisp snap.

Must be amateurs who built this fire. I bet they used green wood and that's why it's smoking.

I heard boys' voices before I saw them, Derek and James. Both boys were juniors like John Ray and both were wearing jeans and Carhartt jackets. They stood hunched over that pitiful fire and were smoking cigarettes. I didn't like them. They were spitters. They'd pull on their cigarettes as they inhaled and then take turns spitting. And they were saggers. Their pants hung loose on their hips and I could see their underwear.

Those two guys sure aren't traditional and they're not even urban. The guys I saw in downtown Minneapolis liked to slouch around with their pants low, but these guys have never been out of the UP. They must think it's cool to have their jeans hang low, but they are so lame. At least they're smoking cigarettes and not pot. I knew what pot smelled like but tonight all I smelled was good ol' cigarettes or "smokes" as some of the old folks call them.

They were both Ojibway, unlike John Ray and myself. Most people don't get it that just because we're Indian, we're not all alike. Different tribes have different customs, traditions and languages. But those two boys and John Ray and myself are alike in a lot of ways because the Potawatomi, Ojibway and Odawa are part of the Three Fires Confederation. Potawatomi means Keepers of the Fire, the sacred and ceremonial fires, and not that lame fire Derek and James had built.

John Ray reached out to touch my shoulder.

"Relax, Cady. It's ok, you're with me. Once they're gone, I want to talk to you about the eagle feather."

"You mean the one I found in school?"

"Yes, that one," he answered.

"But no one but the principal knows about that."

"No, Cady, you're wrong. Someone else knows about it and that person told me. Come on."

I followed him but I was nervous. Eagle feather business is serious.

CHAPTER 2
OSHKODE (FIRE)

We'd left the woods and walked onto a strip of beach about 20 feet by 20 feet. In the center of this area was the fire struggling to stay lit. A ring of blackened rocks, stained by earlier fires, surrounded the pitiful little flames the two guys had built.

Derek and James were puffing on their cigarettes. They offered to share with John Ray but he turned them down. And then I remembered—John Ray doesn't smoke.

"I like doing sports, guys, and Coach would kill me if he knew I'd been doing that stuff," I had overheard him tell his buddies in the school hallway. Everybody at school knew John Ray trained all year and between track and basketball, football, soccer and boxing, he didn't have much time to fool around. The other boys admired him but they'd never admit it.

I don't know why John Ray hangs out out with Derek and James because they're both losers. But I'm the new girl in school and maybe I don't know everything about them. Or maybe it's a guy thing?

"Still smoking, huh, Derek? One of these days I'll get you to quit," John Ray joked. Then he put his hand on my shoulder and squeezed it softly. I leaned in a little to be closer to him. I hoped he'd kiss me but that didn't happen. The others didn't notice. They were too busy arguing about the score of a basketball game. About five minutes passed and then Derek flicked his cigarette into the fire. He nudged James in the shoulder and motioned back to the woods, "Let's get out of here."

"Yeah, time to leave the lovebirds alone. Later, dude," James muttered and straightened up. He paused long enough to give John Ray a fist bump. "Later, bro. Next time we'll bring something to drink." And then, of course, he spit but not at John Ray. He spit like he was marking his territory.

"Yeah, it will be time to paarrr-ty!" Derek added.

The fire was dying but it still cast enough light that I could see the slight snicker on James' face as he and Derek walked off through the woods.

John Ray added a few small branches to the flames.

I was so nervous that I thought I might throw up. I swallowed a few times so I didn't. I was glad I'd only eaten soup and a few crackers for supper. John Ray sat on the log his friends had dragged from the woods. He pointed to a log on the other side of the fire.

"Why don't you sit over there, Cady?"

I hesitated and maybe I even shrunk a little into myself because it hurt that he didn't want me to sit next to him. *What? No kiss?* I tugged at the bottom of my hoodie and pushed a stray lock of hair out of my face before I sat down. I looked down at the ground and picked up a small and smooth brown stone and slipped it into my pocket. I wanted a souvenir of this night, something to look at and touch to help me remember this important night, the night I met John Ray in the woods.

John Ray stood and searched the area until he found a dry piece of wood tucked away a few yards from the fire ring. He threw the log on the fire, and bright flames rose in a brief blaze of orange and yellow before settling down. And this time, the wood made a satisfying crack as it burned. I used the toe of my right shoe to sketch a pattern in the sand. I was trying not to stare at John Ray.

"Cady, I know about the sacred eagle feather you found in school."

He flexed the fingers of one hand into the air as if to pull the words from in front of him. Then he shook his head slightly from left to right and back again. The light from the fire shone on his face and when he realized that I was looking at him, he smiled as if to reassure me.

The eagle feather.

"Oh, yeah, that."

"Yeah, that. Want to talk about it?"

After my third-hour math class had ended yesterday, I was walking down the hallway to my locker when I spotted an eagle feather on the floor. The feather had fallen out of a senior girl's locker. I could tell that the girl hadn't noticed it because she was talking and laughing with her friends. She had slammed her locker shut and walked away, totally ignoring the sacred feather on the floor.

"Loser," I'd mumbled out loud.

I was shocked because my dad had told me that some people believe when an eagle feather falls, it is a bad omen. Some believe it might even mean a warrior has died. It is a great honor to have been given an eagle feather and that girl had disrespected it.

I went to the principal's office and told him about the feather. Our principal is about my height and wears his hair cut short. Traditional people will often cut their hair as a sign of respect and mourning when a loved one passes on. But I think he just liked to wear his hair short and I sure wasn't going to ask him about it. He wore the same clothes every day—a polo shirt, khaki pants and about a ton of keys. You could always hear him coming because of the jingling. He runs most of the time trying to keep up with all the kids. He must wear out a lot of running shoes. He told me to go back down the hallway and not to let anyone touch it. He was going to call a pipe carrier and ask him to remove the feather.

"Do you know what a pipe carrier is?" he asked me.

He was probably trying to be helpful because I was a new kid but it made me mad.

"Of course I know what it is," I almost yelled at him. Sometimes I get mad really fast, probably because I still missed my mom and I wasn't used to Francine being in our house. I loved my new little brother, but he sure did cry a lot at night and I needed my sleep.

"Calm down, Cady. I was only trying to help. You're new here. This probably happened for a reason. Stay alert now, a message might be coming to you from the spirit world. You might be given a special task to complete or a mystery to solve now that you've shown you know about respect and honor. Pay attention to your dreams and watch out for signs."

"You mean like a mystery?"

"Well, sort of. Just pay attention and see what happens."

I left the principal's office, walked back down the hallway and guarded the feather. My dad had once explained to me that a pipe carrier conducts our traditional ceremonies using a sacred pipe. That person is a protector of the pipe and not its owner. The person carrying the pipe shouldn't think negative thoughts and should be free of drugs and alcohol.

About 20 minutes later, the principal and an old man came down the hallway. The older man had long gray hair and was wearing a faded plaid flannel shirt and an old pair of jeans. His boots were patched but polished to a shiny brown. They stopped and the older man picked up the feather and wrapped it in a piece of soft leather. Then he looked at me.

"*Megwetch.*"

He was whispering and I had to lean toward him. His face was sort of weathered and wrinkled, but it reassured me.

He looks kind of like I remember my grandpa.

The principal took me to math class and told my teacher that I'd been with him. On the way there he told me that the elder had taken the feather home and would do a pipe ceremony with it. I'd been taught by my dad and grandma that the pipe connects the earth and the sky. It represents our prayers and its smoke is our words. Once the sacred tobacco or *sema* is placed in the pipe and lit, its smoke carries our prayers to the Creator.

He told me the elder would keep the feather and pass it on someday to a person who deserved it. The girl who had let it fall from her locker had disrespected it. I was still just a kid and she was a senior but I was a lot smarter about some things than she was.

"But, John Ray, how did you find out about the feather?"

"Cady, that pipe carrier was my grandpa. He told my grandma, 'She's done an honorable deed, that girl is a good one. She has much of the traditional ways about her. Not too many like her around anymore.' Even my grandma was impressed and wants to meet you. And then I remembered. You're in Miss Grady's Indian Literature class during sixth hour and I'm in her second-hour class so we've got the same assignment."

"You mean that living history project? We've got to interview an elder and write his or her life story."

"I figured you might need help. I talked it over with my grandma and she agreed to let you interview her. She keeps to herself a lot so this is really a big deal. What do you think, Cady?"

Meeting John Ray in the woods was the most exciting thing to happen to me in my entire life, and I hoped it was because he liked me. I had even hoped he might try to kiss me. And now he was telling me he wanted me to meet his grandma. Do normal guys even do that? Don't they want to kiss you and touch you and fool around or try to get you to drink beer or take pills or something? I didn't think they wanted you to hang out with their grandma. I could hear Irish saying, "Lame, Cady, so lame." But the project was due in two weeks and I needed to earn a good grade. Maybe then my dad would start trusting me again.

"Uh, sure, yeah, that would be great," I stammered. Then I did what I always do when I'm nervous. I pressed the thumb of my right hand into the palm of my left. I squeezed that thumb really hard. It always calmed me. I pressed and squeezed and hoped John Ray didn't notice how nervous I was.

The branches in the fire crackled and then the wind picked up and started to throw bits of ash around. The ashes reminded me of the dream I'd had the night before. In my dream I was using a piece of charcoal to draw in my sketchbook. Bits of charcoal and ashes were scattered everywhere on the carpet. I tried to clean it up but couldn't. Then a blue jay landed on my shoulder and said, "It's there. It happened. Do your best to clean it up and move forward."

Lost in these thoughts, I gazed up at the sky. The moon was shining brighter now.

John Ray stood up and brushed his hands down his pants legs.

"Come on, let's douse this fire. The guys left an old pail here. I'll haul water up from the lake and dump it on the flames. Then I'll race you back to town."

Using our flashlights, we followed the path back through the woods. I started to stumble but caught myself.

Stupid, Cady, stupid. You should have fallen and then John Ray would have helped you up and then you could have collapsed into his arms like they do in the movies.

I wondered of I'd ever be in John Ray's arms. I could almost hear Irish laughing and saying, "*Ney.*"

Chapter 3
Nondede (My Father)

Dad was awake when I got home. He paced back and forth in the living room and waved his hands around. There was a clock on the wall behind him, 9:30.

"Cady, come here. I want to know where you've been!" His words sounded like little bursts of thunder.

"Uh, out," I replied. My legs started to shake, a sure giveaway that I wasn't telling the whole truth. I hated when that happened.

"That's obvious. But where exactly were you when you were out?"

I've got one of those faces that can't cover up the truth. I hate that about myself. When my little cousins ask me if Santa Claus is real, I tell them I don't know and to ask someone else. And then I have to leave the room.

"I thought you knew I went out and that it was okay. You were sleeping on the couch and I didn't want to wake you up," I told him.

And it's not like you ever notice me anymore anyway. But I knew better than to say those words to him. I wasn't stupid.

"You're not getting out of it that easy. When I heard your bedroom door slam shut after supper, I thought you'd gone to your room for the night. Where were you and who were you with? Is that cigarette smoke I smell on you?"

He walked closer to me. He made sniffing noises as he approached.

"I was at the beach with some kids from school. Two of the guys were smoking but I wasn't. That's what you smell."

"And?

"And, that's all. We talked and hung out and then one of them ran back here with me. And now I'm home."

"Cady, I need to know where my kids are, especially at night. Things are different now that Francine and the baby are with us but you're still my kid. You're grounded for the next week. You're to come straight home from school and not leave the house. Have you forgotten what I've told you? Show me who your friends are and I will show you your future."

He grunted but when he added, "Now get to bed," it was as loud and clear as if he'd used a microphone. He picked up the remote control and turned on the television. I had been dismissed.

I ran up to my room so he wouldn't see me cry. I wanted to scream that I hated him but I didn't do it because if I screamed I'd probably wake up my baby brother. Now Dad and Francine would be watching me every minute to make sure I didn't sneak out again.

Everything in my life changed once Dad married Francine and she moved in with us. I really do love my new baby brother. I like to watch him in his crib. He makes the cutest little snuffling sounds and just this week, he discovered his fists and he loves to chew on them. He has fat little cheeks and when I touch one of them, he smiles at me.

It's Francine, my new stepmother, who's caused the bad changes in my life. In my head I call her my stepmonster. She uses her little-girl tricks to get what she wants from my dad. But it usually doesn't take long before her bashful looks and excited squeals turn to fighting and yelling. Their voices grow louder and she yells, "Don't treat me like a little girl. I am your wife and a mother and I'm in charge of this house!"

I want to scream at her, "You chose an old man. Now deal with it. And, if you're so grown up, why do you still wear your long hair braided in pigtails like a little kid?"

It was quieter at home before the baby came. But after Colson was born, after the first few happy days, it became bad again. My dad looks old now. He has bags underneath his eyes and he's gotten fat.

My dad was raised to be a traditional Indian, which means his family followed the old-time ways. He told me he'd grown up in a cabin in the woods in Minnesota. People who weren't Indian made fun of him when he was a little kid because of his long hair but he wouldn't cut it.

He wanted to be a medicine man like his great-uncle and he even trained with him for a year after he graduated from high school. He told me the two of them only spoke in the language and lived in a trailer near a lake somewhere near the border between Michigan and Canada. He spent every day of that year studying and learning from his uncle. He had to memorize everything he learned. They didn't have a television or a radio or even a telephone. They hunted and trapped for their food and heated the trailer with wood.

His great-uncle died and my dad went into the Army because he didn't know what else to do. That's when he stopped being a traditional and studying to be a medicine man. He had to cut his hair because the Army made him but he didn't care anymore. He stayed in the Army until he was hurt and given disability pay. He's good at math which you wouldn't guess because he can never balance a checkbook, but that's only because he likes to spend money and he's always sending money to one of his grown-up kids who are my older brothers and sisters. I don't see them very often. We have different moms and live in different states, but they call him now and then. Usually they need money, so he tries to help them out.

But now all I can think about is meeting up again with John Ray. What if he wants to meet me again at night? How could that happen? I'm grounded for a week and I know Dad and Francine will be watching me.

Chapter 4
Nookomis (Grandmother)

John Ray was waiting for me after lunch the next day at school. It was salad bar day, my favorite. I started with a big serving of lettuce and then I'd added green peppers, cherry tomatoes, onions, shredded ham, and slivers of cheese. I like ranch dressing the best. Liddie, the school cook, is crazy about nuts and thinks kids should eat more of them. Whenever it's salad day, she gives me my own special little dish with cashews and walnut halves and slivered almonds.

"I don't do this for everyone, Cady, but you're a good kid. Besides, your dad is my favorite cousin. Just don't tell the others about this." She gave me a quick hug before going back into the kitchen.

I sat down with Irish at a table in back of the cafeteria and in the middle of things. Kids were talking and laughing. Some were even shouting until a teacher put a stop to it. Three teachers sat at tables in the back with a couple of kids and the shop teacher had a thermos of coffee in front of him. Irish was taking apart her salad.

"This is gross, Cady. Why can't we have pizza or tater tots or tacos or real food? Cows and goats eat salads, not growing kids. At least they didn't run out of chocolate milk today," she grumbled and then used her straw to blow bubbles in the milk until it started to gurgle.

I laughed. I couldn't help it because Irish was such a little kid sometimes. Today she had bunched her hair into five or six little ponytails. She wore her favorite ripped jeans and a pink T-shirt with a picture of a sequin-covered unicorn on it. She loved shopping at the Dollar Store and had about 10 pink-and-white plastic bangle bracelets on each wrist and they made a clacking sound when she moved her hands.

"Anything new I should know about?" Somehow she managed to push the words out between her bubble blowing.

I was dying to tell her about meeting John Ray last night but if I did she'd want to know everything he said. And telling her that he wanted me to meet his grandma was embarrassing. She'd ask me why he'd want to do that. Didn't he want to be alone with me like a normal boy would? Just boy and girl stuff without an old granny sitting there?

"No, not much. Except my dad waits up for me at night now so I have to check in with him if I go out. And I'm grounded for the next week."

"Tough luck. Guess we won't be meeting up at the mall."

The bell rang. We had four minutes to get to our next class.

"Catch you later, girlfriend, gotta bounce." She stood up, grabbed her lunch tray and took off.

I stacked my lunch tray and left the cafeteria. John Ray was waiting for me in the hallway. He wore faded jeans, a washed-out Led Zeppelin T-shirt, an old pair of Nike's and a copper bracelet on his right wrist. He's one of those guys who looks good in whatever he wears. Maybe it's because he's so healthy. I have an older brother, Bruce, who lives in Minnesota and works for Indian Health Services. He buys his clothes at second-hand stores and vintage places and people always want to know where he bought whatever he's wearing because he looks like a model. Bruce usually shrugs and says, "Oh, around."

Chapter 5
Mishiimin (Apple)

I was so excited about seeing John Ray again that I tossed and turned most of that night.

I'd sleep for an hour or two and then wake up and tap at the little digital clock on the table next to my bed. I'd tap it to make it light up so that I could see the time. I'd move the covers around and turn my pillow over and then fall back asleep. When my alarm started buzzing at 6:30, I sat upright. I woke up groggy but excited.

I pulled all my clothes from my closet and threw them on my bed. Some landed in piles on the floor. What do you wear to meet a boy's grandma? A grandma who's an elder? A grandma who people say is crabby? Certainly not an old T-shirt and ripped jeans. I finally chose a pair of dark gray slacks and a white shirt that buttoned down the front. I had worn them last year at my old school's concert and they still fit. I slipped on a pair of brown boots with stacked heels. They made me look older and not like a little girl anymore. I added tiny silver hoop earrings and a silver cuff bracelet that my mom had forgotten to take with her. It had a small dent in it which was why she'd probably left it. I slipped the tobacco pouch for John Ray's grandma into my backpack.

After I showered and dressed, I ran downstairs and grabbed a blueberry granola bar for breakfast. The school bus was coming up to the corner and I ran to catch it. I was in enough trouble at home and I didn't want to make it worse by missing the bus because then I'd be in trouble at school too. The bus was pulling away when I got to the corner but one of the kids started yelling at Gus, the bus driver, to stop. He pulled over and I got on.

Gus was really strict about being on time.

"You've got three minutes, kid. That's all the time I'll wait so you better be there," he told me on that first day I rode the bus. "I almost didn't pull over. You're a lucky kid."

"Only sometimes, Gus," I told him and grabbed a seat.

My dad had driven me out to the rez for the first few days of school but then he stopped.

"Cady, it's 20 miles from town out to your school and then 20 miles back. That's a 40-mile round trip for me each time I take you or pick you up, which adds up to 80 miles a day. That takes up time and gas. You're riding the bus from now on."

The public school was only 8 blocks from our house and I could have walked there but Dad wanted me to go to the reservation school.

"I haven't done a very good job of teaching you about our culture. Your grandma and I think this school will be good for you. They'll teach you your language and history and customs. You might even learn to do beadwork and to like it!"

That was kind of a joke in our family. Everyone did beadwork except me because no one had ever taught me. I had tried to teach myself but my finished pieces were terrible. My stitches were uneven and some were tied too tight and others not tight enough, which meant some of the beads loosened and fell off.

I had culture class at 8:30 a.m. which I sort of liked because I was finally learning to do decent beadwork. Our teacher was named Iris, after the flower. Her sisters were named Rose, Peony, and Petunia, who she said everyone called Toony. My first day in Iris's class she looked at me and announced in a loud voice, "My dad was in the military. That's how I was raised and that's how I live my life."

She was in her early 40s, 5 feet 4 inches tall and stocky with broad shoulders. Her hands were small and her fingers were chubby. She was known all over the powwow circuit for her beadwork. I'd even heard about her before we moved here. She liked to bead vests and decorated the leather with fancy designs of flowers and butterflies.

"I am a true artist. I am not the most spectacular of beadwork artists," she told us at least forty times each day.

She wore glasses, but no makeup. She wasn't much into dressing up, but she knew how to dress a deer. She almost always wore khaki pants and long-sleeved men's shirts buttoned up to the top. Her feet were really tiny and she wore white running shoes until it was winter when she switched it up to brown lace-up boots. There was always a can of soda on her desk. I noticed that because almost everyone I knew in the Upper Peninsula drank coffee.

She was half Potawatomi and half Chippewa, or Ojibway.

"I'm half and half, a real 'Potato Chip,'" she told us the first day of class. She laughed so hard her belly shook and we all laughed with her even though it was a joke we'd all heard for about a million years.

"I grew up on a reservation less than 200 miles from here in Sault Sainte Marie, Michigan. I started learning our traditions from my grandmother when I was just a young child. We follow the Seven Grandfathers and one of those teachings is Respect. I will respect you and I expect you to respect me. Got it?"

She held our attention as she waved her hands in the air. She was barrel-chested and wore her thin brown hair straight and it went past her shoulders.

"In case you're wondering, I consider myself a traditional. I follow the old ways. The only reason I'm wearing khakis is that I have a health problem and wearing pants is easier. But when

I dance in the arena I wear my jingle dress and wave my eagle feather fan with pride."

Jingle dancers had their own special regalia. Their long dresses were covered with metal cones that made a lovely musical noise, or jingle, as they danced. They are known as healing dresses.

"Oh, students, it is a sacred duty to be a jingle dancer. I carry the prayers and sorrows of many when I dance. And as I dance I pray for their healing. We must carry on these traditions and continue to honor them. That is why it is so important you pay attention in this class and learn from myself and the elders I will bring in to teach you."

She talked to us a lot about beadwork, recipes, birds, her pet raccoon, the bear she chased from her back porch, and how to use birchbark when making baskets and earrings. Her class was my favorite because she almost always made me laugh.

After Iris's class, the school day dragged. I couldn't concentrate and I even got that "you better shape up and pay attention" gaze from my social studies teacher. Each hour seemed to last forever. Finally it was almost 2 o'clock.

The bell rang five minutes later and I went to Indian Lit class. We're reading *Night Flying Woman* by Ignatia Broker. It's about *Ni-bo-wi-se-gwe*, which means Night Flying Woman. She was an Ojibway woman who lived in the 19th century in Minnesota and was forced to learn the new ways by white settlers. She was strong enough to hold on to her traditional ways at the same time. I wondered if I could ever be that strong.

At 2:55 p.m. the final bell of the day rang and we went outdoors. John Ray waited for me near the front door.

"Hey, Cady, hurry up. My grandma's waiting." His tone was gentle and it helped to calm me down.

It would have been nice if he told me I looked good but he didn't.

Guess that's only in the movies.

"Come on, we're walking because it's not too far to Grandma's house. Too bad you wore those boots. I'm guessing they're hard to walk in."

"No, they're fine." I thought of what my mom had told me years ago when I was too young to really understand. I was only about five years old but I remembered it clearly. She'd been sitting in her bedroom in front of a lighted make-up mirror and was plucking her eyebrows with a tweezers. She had been startled when I walked into the room.

"Oh, Cady, the things we women do to look good!"

And then she'd laughed with that carefree laugh of hers. I missed her and hoped that she missed me. She had taken off with another guy when I was little and hadn't even said goodbye. I was still mad about that and even though she sent me cards every Christmas and on my birthday, I shoved them in an old shoe box. Maybe someday I'd read them.

Now I wanted to grow up and not be like her. Maybe staying in school and not dropping out like she had would be a good thing. I wanted to have babies someday but not until I was as least thirty. Then I could have a career or something to be proud of. At least interviewing John Ray's grandma would get me a good grade in one of my classes. It was a start.

I followed John Ray across the parking lot and down a paved road leading to a cluster of houses nestled among the trees in back of the school. He stopped in front of a one-story house painted a bright yellow. A small porch stretched across its front and a ramp led down one side of it. He turned to see if I had caught up with him and must have noticed my surprise.

"That ramp was built when my Aunt Betsy was still alive and lived here. But she's gone now."

He then walked up the steps and pounded on the door. He opened it and yelled, "Grandma, it's me and my friend, Cady. Are you home?"

A cheerful-sounding voice answered back, "Of course, where did you think I'd be? Quilting? Playing cards? At bingo? Come on into the kitchen. I'm making applesauce."

The tantalizing aroma of cooking apples, cinnamon, and sugar drew us into the kitchen. And there she was, a medium-sized woman wearing a wrap-around green checked apron over a long denim skirt and a white blouse printed with tiny purple flowers. Her braided gray hair trailed down her back. Her skin was wrinkled from the sun. She was beautiful.

"Hello there. You must be Cady." She pointed to one of the high-backed kitchen chairs.

"Go on, sit down and try a bit of this. I hope you like cinnamon. I think it's a pretty good batch."

I sat down and tried a taste of the applesauce she placed in front of me. "Wow, this is really good," I practically shouted. It was more than good and I savored the contrasting tastes of tart apples, spicy cinnamon, and sweet sugar. It was nice and chunky the way I like it.

"It's really good, ma'am," I told her again.

Her chuckle echoed throughout the kitchen. "Well, I would hope so."

John Ray stood there and beamed at both of us.

"Time for you to go, John Ray. This girl and I have work to do and I don't need you getting in the way. Take that jar of applesauce home to your dad. Go on, scoot now."

He laughed and picked up the jar. The door slammed behind him when he left.

"Just let me finish up this batch and then we'll get to work," his grandma told me. "I found some photos I want to show you."

I watched her back as she stirred a mixture in a large yellow-spotted enamel pot on the stove.

As I sat there in a high-backed wood chair, the fragrant smell of the apples cooking with cinnamon and sugar brought back a memory from long ago. Dad had taken me with him in his truck to visit his folks. I was excited because I liked visiting with my aunties and uncles and cousins. My grandma's house had a big, old-fashioned farm kitchen with lots of counters and windows. It had shelves (bread boards, my grandma called them) that slid out from under the counters. My grandma and my dad's two sisters, Jane and Penny, were with me in the kitchen where they were teaching me to make apple pies.

They'd already peeled the apples and had me sit at the kitchen table with my woman's knife that my Uncle Jack had made for me. The blade was made of obsidian and measured less than four inches in length. The handle was made from polished orange wood in the shape of a small tusk and was tied to its blade with a piece of sinew, which is like a leather string. Uncle Jack had made the knife for me as a surprise for my ninth birthday. My grandma and aunties had covered the old formica-topped kitchen table with a vinyl cloth and put a wooden board in front of me. They'd made a big deal out of giving me the knife, which was small enough to fit my hand perfectly.

Then they'd put a small wooden cutting board (shaped like an apple!) in front of me. They showed me how to cut an apple using my new knife.

"Use it like a saw, Cady. Don't slice the apple, saw it," my auntie instructed me.

I had moved that little knife back and forth until I'd managed to cut a few slices of apple without cutting myself. I was happy and felt like a grown-up, but it was taking me forever.

"Cady, let's put that knife away for now. We'll get it out again someday when you're older," Grandma told me.

Then my Auntie Jane told me to use her paring knife. She explained that a paring knife is a small knife used to cut fruit or vegetables. Her paring knife had a pretty white pearl handle for me to grip.

"Best to put your new knife in its sheath so you don't cut yourself or anyone else," she told me.

My uncle had put the sheath together out of leather using whip stitches. It had a little row of fringe up its side. The best part was that he'd cut slits in the back of the sheath so that I could slip a belt through it.

"Your uncle worked hard on making that knife for you and loaded it up with prayers so that it would serve you wel,l but we'll put it aside for now so that we can finish these pies," she added. That was such a happy memory and I hoarded it like a squirrel hoards a stash of nuts.

John Ray's grandma moved the pot off the stove and hit its side with a large wooden spoon. The sound startled me and I almost tipped over the glass of water on the table in front of me.

"There, done for today. Come on now, let's move into the front room. I understand you want to interview me?"

"Yes, ma'am," I replied. I almost knocked a chair over in my nervous rush to leave that fragrant kitchen.

She sat down in the middle of a large brown couch and patted the cushion next to her.

"Why don't you join me here? Then, when your questions are done, I have some photos to show you. And, Cady, you can call me Grandma Eunice."

And then I remembered the gift my dad had told me to give her. I opened my backpack and pulled out the leather pouch filled with *sema* or tobacco.

"This is for you," I told her and handed it to her.

"Thank you," she said and accepted my offering. A smile danced around her lips.

The next two hours passed by quickly. I'd brought a notebook with me in my backpack and had written out a list of questions during my study hall earlier that afternoon. I wrote down Grandma Eunice's answers. It was a good thing she was a slow talker. Actually, it wasn't that she talked slowly. It was that she liked talking. Each of her answers was like she was telling me a story. Now I know why John Ray and his family were known as storytellers.

We were almost done when she showed me the old photographs.

"I wanted you to know what this reservation used to be like. It wasn't like it is now with these nice houses and paved roads. We didn't even have electricity here until 1967!"

I hadn't been born in 1967 and then it hit me. For her, 1967 wasn't that long ago. I guess she didn't realize that I was only 13 or else she'd forgotten it.

"Here's a photo of all of us back then. This was taken after the first electric lights were put in."

As I leaned over, a colored photo slipped out from the small stack of black and white ones on the table and fell on the floor. I picked it up and I stared at the beautiful woman shown there who must have been in her early 20s. She wore a long skirt and blouse and her hair was almost waist-length. Her only jewelry was a necklace. I examined it more closely and noticed it was made of small, almost tiny, white shell beads. Larger pieces of turquoise and jade were spaced along its length and dangling from its center was a carved white bear. He stood upright on his two legs. His front paws were folded at his chest. Two tiny black eyes glowed.

"Is there a story behind this necklace?" I pointed to the woman in the middle of a group of six young women. "Why is she wearing that necklace?"

Grandma Eunice stood suddenly and grabbed the photo from my hand and placed it back into the stack. She put the stack into a large brown envelope.

"That's enough for today. I've got dinner to make for John Ray's grandpa. Your ride back to town should be here any minute now." She walked out of the room.

I shivered and searched for my jacket. Brakes squealed as the bus pulled up in front.

Grandma Eunice came back into the living room, walked to the front door and opened it. She was frowning as she stood there and held my jacket out to me.

I crossed to the door, thanked her for the interview, turned and walked down the porch.

I got onto the bus wondering what had happened. Why had she taken that photo out of my hand? Had it meant she didn't approve of me? Would she tell John Ray? What if she told him not to talk to me anymore?

I tried not to but I started to cry. I brushed my tears away with my hand but they kept falling. I wanted John Ray's grandma to like me and she did at first. But then, when I asked her about the necklace, she had practically pushed me out of there.

I dug around in my backpack for my journal. I wanted to draw a sketch of the necklace I'd seen in the photo at Grandma Eunice's. My old-style cell phone didn't have a photo app that worked and there hadn't been time to take a photo anyway. She grabbed that photo from me so fast!

What was going on? Why was this mystery showing up in my life? Didn't I have enough to do trying to fit in at a new school? Wasn't it hard enough at home just getting along with Dad and Francine?

And now a mystery was showing up in my life and John Ray's grandma was part of it.

Why had Grandma Eunice grabbed that photo out of my hand? The principal warned me I might be given my very own mystery to solve. Was this it?

Chapter 6
Makwa (Bear)

Later that night, after I had washed the supper dishes and taken the garbage out, I went upstairs to my room. My bedroom was the smallest room in our house. It had only one window but at least I could open it during the warmer months. When it was only two of us, Dad slept on the couch in the living room and I had the other bedroom, the big one down the hall, to myself. He had used this little room as his workroom but now that he married again, he shared the big bedroom with Francine and the baby. I didn't want to think anymore about that.

My bed took up most of the small bedroom's space. When I moved into this room its walls had been covered with an ugly brown and green wallpaper. It had pictures of little clocks and teapots on it. I hated it so I talked Dad into helping me paint over it. I picked out an amazing purple color but Dad thought it was too dark.

"Cady, you are old enough now to learn about compromise."

So that's what we did. We compromised on a white color with a lot of lilac overtones or undertones or something.

The old overhead light was in the shape of a teapot so we replaced it with a big white paper lantern from the Dollar Store. It made the room seem grown up and it gave more light. Bugs didn't get caught in it like they did in the old light. I know bugs are living creatures and part of Mother Earth, but I still don't like them in my bedroom.

Next to my bed was a little wooden cupboard with three drawers. The best part was that the bottom drawer locked. My room wasn't big enough for a desk so I sat on my bed when I did my homework. I'd put a red reading lamp on top of the cupboard for more light.

My closet was crammed with T-shirts and jeans, a few pairs of shoes and my moccasins, worn-out boots and old books and papers. Sometimes, if I forgot and opened the door without standing in a certain way, things would fall off the top shelf and land on my head. I dreamed about having a walk-in closet someday.

I wanted to go outdoors and go running but I was still grounded so I did the next best thing. I liked to straighten things and clean things when I've got thinking to do. I kept thinking about how John Ray's grandma had changed. She had been nice and friendly and had answered almost all of my questions. Then, after the photo fell out of the pack, she'd gotten quiet and told me it was time to leave. What had happened?

I picked up my clothes from the closet floor, dumped them on the bed and sorted them into clean and dirty piles. The dirty clothes would go into the hamper in the hallway. I started hanging up the cleaner ones in the closet when I stubbed my toe against something.

A small strip of carpet was sticking up. I tore at the small strip and it made a satisfying "zrrrp" and dust filled the air. Strips of wood, about two inches wide, had been used as floorboards. One of the boards didn't match. It was a light brown and the others were almost black. I lifted up that board and discovered a hollowed-out space about four inches by four inches. Inside I found a small bag of faded leather. I pulled it it out and loosened its cord and shook out a necklace. It was the same necklace I had seen in the photo at Grandma Eunice's!

I dug around in my backpack for my journal. On the bus ride home yesterday I'd sketched a picture of the necklace in the photo. I held the necklace against my drawing and they were almost an exact match. It had to be the same necklace!

33

The beads were like miniature white pebbles with holes drilled through the middle so they could be strung. The necklace was a double strand and also held tiny sapphire blue and light green stones. It even had a white stone bear.

My Indian name, the name the spirits know me by, is *Mkos Kwe* or Little Bear Woman. When the medicine man had given me this name, he told me, "This is a healing name. Honor it." And now I found a bear dangling from a necklace. And I found it hidden under my closet floor.

I'd been taught that when something shows up in your life like this it is for a reason.

Why had the necklace appeared to me in the photo and now in my closet? Is this a message of some kind? Who did the necklace belong to and who hid it here?

I made a list of people I could talk to about it and wrote their names in my notebook. My dad, Irish, my teachers, John Ray, and then I crossed each of them off the list except John Ray. I wanted to show him the necklace and tell him that a beautiful woman in one of his grandma's old photos was wearing the same necklace. I would ask him if she would help me. I needed his grandma to answer these questions. She was nice to me at first but then she became a little crabby and a little scary. I needed John Ray to be my go-between.

I put the necklace back into its leather pouch and hid it under the floorboard where I'd found it.

Chapter 7
Naabikaagan (Necklace)

John Ray was standing next to my locker the next day. It was just before the bell for our first class.

"Hey, Cady, how was your interview with my grandma yesterday?"

I nudged him aside and opened the locker door. I grabbed my history book before slamming the door shut.

"Not that great. I mean, she was really nice to me at first and answered almost all of my questions. And she didn't treat me like a little kid and I liked that. But when she was showing me some old photos, one fell out of the pile. I picked it up and was looking at it and she practically grabbed it from my hand. Then she told me it was time for me to leave and she was kind of crabby about it."

"Cady, that doesn't sound like my grandma. Why would she do that? Especially since she knows you're my friend."

"Yeah, and there's more, but I can't talk about it now. I've got class in a few minutes."

"Let's meet up later at the coffee shop across the street from the library in town. How about at 4:00?"

A coffee shop? I'd never been to a coffee shop and I don't even drink coffee. Is this what older boys do? Do they drink coffee and meet up with other kids in coffee shops?

But then he smiled that crazy sweet smile of his and his eyes met mine. It was as if the sun was coming up inside of me. I no longer cared that I didn't drink coffee. Of course I'd meet

John Ray. I'd meet him wherever and whenever he wanted, even if I was grounded. I'd take my chances on slipping in at home later and no one noticing that I was late.

"Uh, sure, that'd be ok."

"See you later, Cady." He headed off down the hallway.

I rode the school bus home that day. Our bus driver, Gus, kept to a pretty tight schedule and I got home about 3:30 p.m. I dropped my backpack on the kitchen floor and raced up to my room. I shut the bedroom door and went to the closet where I loosened the board and removed the small leather pouch with the necklace inside. I put the pouch inside the kangaroo pocket in the front of my hoodie.

"Cady, is that you? Are you home?"

"Yeah, Dad, I'm coming," I told him. I took the back stairs down into the kitchen where he was making a fresh pot of coffee.

"Dad, I need to go out. I know I'm still grounded, but I need to go to the library to do some research for one of my classes."

"Just this once you can go, but only if you're home in time for dinner. I'm trying out a new meatloaf recipe and your stepmother should be home from your little brother's checkup at the doctor's by then. And, Cady, you better be home by 5:30. I mean it. Remember, you're still grounded," he reminded me.

As if I haven't heard it a million times. Does he want me to tattoo it on my arm so I won't forget?

"Sure, Dad. Love you, bye," I told him and raced out the back door.

And, once again, I ran. But it was a short run of less than one mile to the public library in Barnesville. The coffee shop, Java Beans, was across the street from the library and tucked between a tattoo parlor and a bike shop. I slowed down the last block or so. I didn't want to be flushed or sweaty when I met John Ray.

When I opened the door, the little bell above the shop's door made a cling-clang-cling. Coffee scents tasting of cinnamon and vanilla filled the air. Chocolate chip cookies were baking and my stomach grumbled. a little with hunger. *Maybe coffee shops aren't so dumb after all.* The shop's few customers glanced up from their conversations or laptops. John Ray was sitting in a booth in the back corner and I walked over to him.

I sat down and he asked, "Do you want coffee or something? I'm buying."

"Well, the thing is, I don't really drink coffee. I'm kind of a soda girl, ginger ale actually."

"One ginger ale coming up. You want the kind they make here in town, right?"

"Of course."

John Ray drank his coffee with a little cream and lots of sugar. I was relieved he didn't order one of those fancy coffee drinks with whipped cream and caramel and stuff. My dad and my older brother drank their coffee the same way John Ray did and that reassured me.

I poured the cool ginger ale into a tall, frosted glass. The golden-colored soda bubbled and fizzed as it hit the ground ice. I ripped the paper covering off the straw and took a first sip. I started to relax.

Is this a date or are we just hanging out? The ginger ale tasted so tart and icy after my run that I almost didn't care. I just wanted to keep d rinking it. Don't slurp, Cady. Manners, manners.

"So, Cady, what was it you wanted to talk to me about?" John Ray fiddled with a stack of paper napkins and had already bunched a few of them into a ball on the table.

"This." I pulled the leather pouch from my pocket and showed him the necklace.

"Where did you get that?" His voice had changed and he sounded nervous.

"I found it hidden under the floor in my closet. I noticed this same necklace in that photo at your grandma's. She wanted me to leave after that. Your family is known for its storytelling. Is there a story that goes with this necklace? Is that why your grandma clammed up on me and refused to talk about the photo? Does it have something to do with the necklace?"

One of John Ray's feet started to tap the floor and then it stopped. He touched my outstretched hand and I handed him the necklace. He took it, turned it over, and then handed it back to me.

"Put it away, Cady. Quick, stick it back in your pocket."

Sweat started to form on the back of my neck. "Not until you tell me what's going on. What's this all about and why was this necklace hidden under the floorboard in my closet? And why did your grandma clam up on me and grab the photo from me? Does it have something to do with the necklace?"

"All I know is that your necklace is special. I'm pretty certain your necklace is the one in my grandma's photo. Your necklace's pendant and the one in the photo both have a little chip in the bear's left paw. But it's something no one talks about." He placed both his hands flat on the table. "That's all I know."

"Why not?" I thought he knew more but wasn't going to tell me and that upset me. Sometimes my temper flares up. It used to get me in trouble a lot. Like the time I slammed the front door of our house so hard that the window broke. I was grounded for two weeks after that.

"Cady, I told you. I don't know why. And I was always too scared to ask." And then his left foot started tapping the floor again.

"You. Scared?" I was stunned.

"Yeah, me, scared. When it comes to my grandma...she can get pretty scary. When she doesn't want to talk about something she can be fierce, trust me." And this time his palm slammed down. "Sorry, I didn't mean to do that."

38

"John Ray, what do I do about all of this? Do I stick the necklace back under the floor and pretend I never found it?"

He took a long drink of his coffee and gazed into the space above my head. A few moments passed.

"Cady, the necklace came to you for a reason. It's like when a person receives a dream. You can't make it happen; if you're meant to receive one, you will. That's what our elders say. And you saw that photo for a reason and you found the necklace for a reason. It came to you, Cady, and not to me. It's up to you to find out what to do about it. I can help you if you want me to and you can talk to me about it and I won't tell anyone else but it's up to you. This is your mystery to solve. This is how it works."

I should have been nervous then, but I wasn't. Even my shoulders loosened up a bit. I'd been taught that when things come to you like this you must respond. This was my test to prove that I was growing up and ready to handle more responsibility. I also wanted to prove to my dad that he could trust me and that I wasn't a little kid anymore. And then maybe things would go back to the way it was be between us. Maybe he'd want to spend more time with me like he used to.

"This is a mystery, isn't it? This is something I need to to do to prove myself."

"Right, Cady. Hey, the library's across the street. Maybe you could start there. Some of the old books might be able to tell you something about your necklace."

It wasn't the dumbest idea. I wanted to get started on this as soon as possible. And then a bird chirped.

"Is there a bird in this coffee shop?"

John Ray pointed to a clock hanging above the cash register. The clock had pictures of different birds covering it. I'd seen these clocks on television commercials and knew that a bird chirped each hour. This time, a blue jay squawked.

"It's 5 o'clock, Cady. We've got a clock like that one at home."

I had barely enough time to run home for dinner. "See you tomorrow?" I tried to sound confident but I wasn't sure I pulled it off.

"For sure."

For a moment I forgot about the necklace. All I could think about was that John Ray wanted to see me again. Me, Cady, the new girl at school. He wants to see me!

I glanced up at that crazy bird clock and realized I only had 30 minutes to run 10 blocks.

"Bye, John Ray, I've got to go."

"*Bama pi*, Cady." *Bama pi* means "until we meet again," because there's no word for goodbye in the language.

I walked out of the coffee shop's door and didn't even turn around to see if John Ray was still there. I was already grounded and I didn't want to get into more trouble. For some dumb reason, I had worn a pair of old flats and not my running shoes and I knew they would slow me down. Now I would have to hurry if I wanted to be home in time for dinner.

And once again there was a blue jay making cawing noise and this time, it was a real bird perched on the top branch of an oak tree across the street.

"Okay, okay, I hear you. Why don't you quit making that racket and help me make it home on time?"

That crazy bird must have heard me because he flew off the branch into the air heading in the direction of my house. I followed him and crossed my fingers.

Chapter 8
Diindiisí (Blue Jay)

~~~~~~~~~~~~~~~~

The next day, I got my dad's approval to go to the library straight from school for research.

"Where would I find books about Indian heritage?" The reference librarian picked her glasses up from the counter and fit them over the bridge of her nose.

"Are you looking for anything in particular?" she responded.

I told her I was interested in Indian jewelry especially the older stuff. Maybe from about 50 or more years ago. I hoped I could find my mystery necklace in one of the old history books.

"Oh, well, in that case, you don't want genealogy. You want our reference section. Follow me and I'll show you."

The library was a great place if you liked books. The Welcome Wagon lady had visited us our first week in town and that's when I learned about it.

"Here are some forms to fill out for library cards," she told Dad.

He filled the cards out after she left. "You can go anytime, Cady. It's important you get a good education and reading will help you do that."

Later that week I walked to the library and explored the different rooms. The inside of the library still had the original light fixtures. They looked like fancy chandeliers and threw a soft yellow light. Most overhead lights make a buzzing, humming sound but these didn't. My favorite part was the children's section. It even had a real boat big enough for two little kids to climb into and play and pretend they were sailing somewhere.

41

I followed the librarian to the second floor. At the top of the stairs and off to the right side was a row of bookshelves. Above them was an old-fashioned wooden sign with antique-type letters that spelled out Reference. On my earlier visit to the library I had only explored the first floor.

"Not many people visit our reference area since the Internet. You might try this section." She bent down and pointed at a middle shelf. "Try these books with the green covers; they might help you. I'll be downstairs if you need me."

I picked up the three books she'd pointed out. *Indian Jewelry* was stamped on the cover and binding of each. I sat down on the floor and started paging through them one by one. The first book was about the history of beadwork in Michigan, Wisconsin, and Minnesota. The second was about earrings, bracelets, hair ties, barrettes and ornaments for decorating dance regalia. It had pictures and photos of beaded moccasins, cuffs, chokers, arm bands and belts. Some people even beaded their eagle feather fans. The beadwork covered the bottom of the fan where the feathers were held together.

Some of the designs were basic, almost plain, and some were more detailed. I pulled my sketchbook from my backpack to copy my favorite. I had started beadwork lessons and wanted to copy this pattern. I was learning to make decent stitches. But my favorite part was still drawing the patterns. My sketch book was filled with sample designs and now I was learning how to transfer them to graph paper using colored pencils. I liked my art classes because sketching came easily to me. Our instructor told us it was important to set goals and to challenge ourselves. Beadwork was definitely more challenging to me than the art classes I had taken at my old school.

I started paging through the third book. It had at least twenty color photos and drawings of necklaces. One or two looked like my necklace but when I examined each more closely, I realized that the ornament dangling from the center was an eagle or a wolf and not a bear.

Then, on the next-to-last page, was a photograph of six women standing in a row. They stood straight with their hands behind their backs. Each wore her long hair piled on top of her head. Their skirts were long and covered their shoes, hitting the floor. A beautiful young woman, second from the left in the photo, was wearing my necklace!

I stood up and carried the book to a nearby window for more light. I dug out my dad's old magnifying glass from my backpack. It was only about five inches long and had an almost worn-out brown leather handle. I had found it in an old box in our basement and kept it in a little zippered pocket in my backpack. I brought the picture closer to my face. Yes, it was my necklace! And then I noticed the hole underneath the photo where the description should have been. Someone had carefully cut out a square about two inches by four inches. Even though I had found a photo of my necklace, there was no information to go with it.

Now what? I was back to square one. I wanted to scream but covered my mouth before I made a sound. Losing my temper wouldn't help. I counted to 10, taking deep breaths to calm myself. And that's when I heard that crazy blue jay noise, *jaay-jaay*. I spun around. *Did they actually have one of those bird clocks in the library?*

No, that wasn't it. Someone had left a window open at the far end of the room and through the window's screen I could see a blue jay perched on the ledge.

What was going on? First, there was the blue jay sound made by the clock in the coffee shop and then a real live blue jay had followed me home. And now this crazy bird seemed to want to tell me something. Was this a sign?

The old ones say if something appears to you three times, you should start paying attention. What was that bird trying to tell me?

Chapter 9
Fry Bread

～～～～～～

The next day after lunch I had polished off two bowls of chili and was eating a saltine cracker when John Ray came over to our table.

"So, Cady, did you find out anything at the library?"

I looked up at him. "Umm, not really." Then I told him about finding the book in the reference section with the photo and the missing information.

"That's weird," he muttered.

"I really don't know," I repeated over and over until the bell rang and we both left for our classes.

Nothing much seemed to happen during the next few days. It was the second week of May and my little brother got his first tooth. May was *Waawaaskone-Giizis*, or the Flower Moon, the fifth moon of Creation. I'd been taught that during the Flower Moon, the plants would send out positive energy to all of us on Turtle Island, the land we stand on. This powerful medicine would help to heal Mother Earth. I hoped it would help me solve my mystery.

John Ray and I weren't going together but something was happening between us. Yesterday afternoon, I was in one of my school's restrooms. Someone had written on the wall of the stall that John Ray and I were hooking up. We were close but it wasn't like that. I grabbed a marker out of my back pocket and crossed it off, and, then I smiled. One week ago I'd met him at the park for the first time. I put my finger to my face on the spot he'd touched when he'd brushed the hair out of my eyes. I didn't wash my face for two days after that! And then he'd put out the fire and we'd raced each other back to town.

I'm not made of stone. I'm a real live girl and I'd like John Ray to kiss me someday and to think of me the way a boy does when he has a girlfriend. But for now, we weren't like that. He was always busy with sports and family things.

Dad had eased up on me and I wasn't grounded anymore so I'd started running again. I ran in town in my neighborhood. I ran to the mini-mart to pick up milk or bread for my dad and stepmom. I ran with the paperboy when he pedaled his bike on his route. He had a hard time keeping up with me.

I found an old stopwatch in the junk drawer in the kitchen and had my dad show me how to use it.

"What do you need this for, Cady? Don't tell me you're going to finally start timing your showers?" he joked. "Do you have any idea how high our water bills are here?" he had thrown this question at me more than once. "Cady, I'm not made of money. When I was in the Army, three minutes for a shower seemed like a long time."

He thought a three-minute shower was long enough but I liked at least 10 minutes. We compromised on four minutes. I'm not kidding. He set the kitchen timer and I had four minutes.

I took four-minute showers when he was home and really long ones when he was gone.

"I need the stopwatch to time my runs," I told him. "As long as I'm running, I might as well see if I can cut my time."

I asked for a new pair of running shoes because I'd outgrown my old ones. My dad took me to the Plaza Mall and I tried on about 20 different pairs before settling on a pair of Nike's. They cost over $100, which in our family is a lot of money. Especially with a new baby in the family and everything he needed. But my dad surprised me.

"I had this money tucked away for a special day and today's that day. If my girl wants to run then she's going to run," he declared as he paid for the shoes. I tried talking him into adding a Nike track suit, (a deep blue with a silver streak down the side of the leg), but that didn't go over too well.

"Cady, enough." It wasn't his words but the tone he used. Enough was enough.

So, I was running and now I was running with decent shoes. I found out that if I took the first bus home from school, I could be out running by 3:30 p.m. Three days later, on a Saturday morning, I was eating my Cheerios at the kitchen table and Dad was pouring himself another cup of coffee. Francine was feeding the baby, who was sitting in his highchair and laughing. Francine had cut bananas into little pieces and he liked to gum them. Then he'd throw some pieces on the floor and mash the others into his bib.

Great, someone's going to have a real mess to clean up.

"Cady, what about your necklace? What have you found out?" I had showed the necklace to Dad one night when he had come into my room to say goodnight. That's when I told him about Grandma Eunice's photo and the one I found in the library.

I looked up from the floor where I was wiping up mashed bananas.

"Nothing, Dad, nothing at all," I muttered.

"Well, I don't know anything about a necklace. Could someone please tell me? For Pete's sake, I'm part of this family now and I'd like to know what this is about," Francine added.

"Better go and get it and show it to her," Dad directed. "But, Francine, it's Cady's necklace. She found it and now she needs to know why she found it. It's her mystery and I have a feeling it's part of her coming of age. Right, kiddo?"

"Whatever you say." I went upstairs and retrieved the necklace from its hiding place in the closet.

Great. Now another person knows about it and a lot of help she'll be. Not.

But Francine surprised me. "It's interesting, Cady, but it's not my style. You can keep it."

What? I could keep it! Francine still had so much to learn. I was only 13 but I knew that when something came to a person then it was up to that person to figure out why. I would not have given it to her even if she begged me. But I was relieved she didn't want it.

"Thanks, Francine." I put the necklace in my pocket and finished cleaning up the banana mess on the floor.

Between school and running, I didn't have much spare time. Things at home had calmed down and my baby brother was finally sleeping through the night. We were all sleeping better now which helped my dad and Francine and me to get along better.

But I wasn't any closer to solving the mystery of why I had found the necklace. I tried not to think about it but it bothered me. Why it had been hidden under my closet floor? What was the mystery surrounding it? Why did John Ray's grandma not want to talk about it? I was doing what I always did when something bothered me. I was procrastinating. The dictionary says procrastination means to delay or put off doing something. I was procrastinating by doing homework and wiping up messy kitchen floors. I was dragging my heels by using my time to go running instead of learning about my necklace.

Later that day, my dad found me in the living room, playing with Colson. The television set was turned down low. The weatherman was predicting rain that night but only an inch or two. The baby was jumping in his jumpy seat and squealing with delight each time he managed to ring the little bells running across the front of the chair. His little cheeks were rosy from teething. When he wasn't hitting the little bells, he was busy chewing on his fist.

"Cady, be sure to be here for dinner tonight. I'm moving it back to 6:30. Your older brother is visiting from Minnesota and I'm planning a special meal. How does pot roast and mashed potatoes sound to you?"

"And fry bread?" I added.

"Now, Cady, don't start with that."

"Okay," I laughed. But I knew that if Bruce was coming for dinner, there would be fry bread. I love fry bread more than anyone else in the family.

There are different stories about fry bread. It has to do with how when our people were first removed to the reservations, they were basically starving. Many times they only had flour and grease and if they had meat it usually wasn't very good. So they invented fry bread. You use flour and a little sugar and milk and mix it with either baking power or yeast. Dad and Bruce always use quick-rise yeast. Let the dough rise and then make it into little balls which you pat and stretch out until it's about one-quarter inch thick. Then you poke a hole in the center with your finger and fry it in hot oil until it's golden brown on both sides. Drain on paper towels. Some people use it instead of taco shells for tacos but I like to eat it with butter and sprinkled with cinnamon sugar. People like to brag about who makes the best fry bread.

It was almost like a party at dinner that night. We feasted on pot roast and mashed potatoes and fry bread. Bruce had brought a seven-layer chocolate cake from a bakery in Minneapolis and we laughed and and Dad told us stories about the old days.

When Dad talks about playing ball back when he was young he looks happy. Maybe his life hasn't been easy. Maybe he's had problems along the way. Is that why he's so quiet sometimes? Is that why he gets moody? Maybe he really has been sick and maybe he really does worry about supporting us.

"Say, Dad," Bruce began, "how about if Cady visits me this weekend for the big powwow? She could ride back with me and stay with me. I'd take her around to meet some of the old folks and I'd make sure she got on the bus safely for the trip home."

"I think that might work out," Dad replied. "Francine and I have been wanting to take the baby to visit her family in southern Wisconsin. This would be a good chance to do that. You'd keep a close eye on your sister, son?"

"Of course, Dad," Bruce's foot nudged mine under the table.

So it was settled. I would be going to Minneapolis and the powwow with Bruce.

I loved my brother and I loved powwows. And maybe I'd meet someone there who could help me solve they mystery of my necklace.

I hadn't forgotten about it. I took it out of its hiding place almost every day and reassured myself that it still existed.

What's your story? I'd whisper as I held it in my hand. The little bear gazed back at me as if to say it was for me to find out and then I would know.

Know what? What will I know?

I'd then ask myself what to do next and where to go for more information. Silence was always my answer. But now I knew. I'd take the necklace with me and visit the vendor booths at the powwow and see what I could find out. There were always artists and craftspeople at powwows. Someone would have to know something about the history of my necklace and what it meant.

Chapter 10
Powwow

~~~~~~~~

The next three days passed in a blur. It was the second week of May with only two weeks until the end of the school year and our teachers were loading on the assignments. We had a major unit test in math and a frog dissection in science. First we practiced with a trial dissection online and then we did an actual dissection. Mine was a female frog and when I cut her open all these eggs fell out, I felt sad for that poor old dead frog. I also had an essay due in English class and a beadwork design to finish for culture class.

I'd rewritten my interview of John Ray's grandma about four times before I turned it in to be graded. I wanted to stop after three but four is a sacred number in our culture. I went to Indian Lit class that Monday in the third week in May and tried to cover my nervousness by kidding around with the others. Eddie was sailing paper airplanes around the room, which I thought was lame and childish. Corina was handing out gum to everybody and saying, "Come on, come on, let's see who can blow the biggest bubble." And then someone would blow a humongous bubble and she'd take a photo of it with her cell phone and laugh. Summer couldn't come soon enough for us.

The bell rang and Miss Grady walked into the room and it suddenly got very quiet. That happened a lot in Indian Lit class because we liked Miss Grady. She didn't teach down to us. She taught us like we were smart enough to figure things out for ourselves.

"Well, students, I have your papers here and overall I'm quite pleased with them.

"You showed great resourcefulness in choosing the elders to interview and by that I mean that not one of you interviewed the same person. Well done.

"And some of you have actually been listening in class because the questions you asked show a great deal of thought. Remember, this assignment counted as your unit exam."

She walked up and down the aisles handing back our papers and saying "Good work" or "Nicely done."

She stopped when she reached my desk.

"Cady, please stay after class. We need to talk." Those words hung suspended in the air while my stomach dropped down to my feet. My hands felt sweaty.

The bell rang and the other kids cheered and grabbed their backpacks and rushed out of the room into the hallway. I sat in my desk and tried not to slump over. *What was this about? Was I in trouble?* Once the others had left, Miss Grady approached my desk. She laid a hand on my shoulder and then sat down in a nearby student desk.

She really is a pretty woman. It's not only her hair or her eyes but it's the way she treats people. She's smart but doesn't brag about it or show off. She's curious about things and likes to learn. I wish more people were like that.

"Cady, relax. I wanted to tell you how much I enjoyed reading your interview. Grandma Eunice is someone I've respected for the 15 years I've been teaching here. I've given this assignment out often and no one else has ever managed to interview her. How did that happen?"

"Oh, uh, a friend helped me," I told her.

"I'm very pleased with the work you've done here but I'm still surprised she agreed to be interviewed. She's changed since... oh, never mind." Just then the timer sounded on her phone.

"My goodness, it's late. You better catch your bus. Good work, Cady." With that she stood up and handed me my paper. A large *A* was written in bright purple ink at the top of the page. And next to that she'd written, "You've heard the words. May you walk into their meaning." Teachers could be mysterious, I thought to myself.

I showed my paper to Dad and Bruce. That night Dad cooked pork chops, mashed potatoes, creamed corn, and chocolate pudding for dessert. He learned to cook when he was in the Army and he enjoys it.

"It's important to love what you do and to put love into your cooking," he used to say. "My mother, your grandmother, taught me that." He still was the main cook in our house because Francine said he was a better cook.

Two years ago, before he met Francine, he went to the casino and played bingo. He usually played video poker but that night he plunked down $10 for 10 bingo cards and a dabber. And he won the grand prize—a brand new computer and printer! He's really good at computer work, probably because he worked with codes in the Army. I know this because I found some old papers of his. There was a space to be filled in describing occupation. Dad had written cryptology. I googled it and it means codes.

I wonder how many kids my age know about the Navajo Code Talkers and how they saved us during World War II. The Code Talkers served in the Marines from 1942 to 1945. They used the Navajo language to send out information about troop size, troop movements and other information the Allied forces needed. It was even faster than using Morse code! And one of the reasons it worked was that fewer than 30 non-native persons understood the language.

Dad brought the computer home after he won it and plugged it in and stayed up all night installing programs and stuff. He taught himself to design websites and started earning extra money. And that's how he met Francine. She used to work at a donut shop and she had talked her boss, Mr. Barley, into having a website made for the shop. Mr. Barley hired my dad, who met there with him and Francine and the rest is history.

After Colson was born, Francine quit selling donuts. Now she stays home with Dad and the baby. I miss the free donuts she'd bring home every Saturday. Dad likes the blueberry ones and I like the puffy ones with caramel frosting. Francine likes anything filled with whipped cream. She's gained a lot of weight since she got together with my dad and I don't think it's because she had a baby. I told her she should take up running but that made her mad.

"Running? Me? Are you crazy, Cady? I've got a baby to take care of," was her reply.

I haven't given up on her. I've been talking to my dad about buying one of those strollers for pushing a baby when you run. I've seen them for sale at rummage sales.

But now I had to focus on my packing. I'd stay with Bruce in his apartment so I wouldn't have to pack too much extra stuff. He's 5 feet 10 inches tall so he's only two inches taller than me. If I forgot something I could always borrow a pair of his jeans or a T-shirt. He'd have towels and sheets and stuff.

I took my old canvas bag off its hook on the back of my bedroom door. It was one my mom had bought at the mall when I was in kindergarten and she still lived with us. It was dark red with a really cool pattern of lightning bolts and stuff. When I'm older and have my own money, I'll replace it with a Pendleton one but this one will do for now. I rolled up some T-shirts, jeans, socks, and underwear and my new running shoes and running gear. I also packed my favorite coconut shampoo, which I knew Bruce wouldn't have.

A T-shirt, sweater, jeans, and my denim jacket would be warm enough at the powwow. It was already the middle of May and the weather was warmer but the powwow would be outdoors somewhere. In northern Minnesota the weather could be cold or warm or even hot in May. Dad promised he'd give me $40 for spending money and I knew Bruce would feed me. Bruce and I were close. He'd lived with us until I was six and then he'd left for college.

I took the necklace from its hiding place in my closet. It was too valuable to pack in my duffle bag. I unwrapped the little pouch's leather thong and fashioned it into a long loop. I'd wear the bag around my neck and keep the necklace close to my heart where it would be safe.

Bruce and I left early the next morning in his sort-of-new car.

"How do you like my pony?" That was our family joke; we called our cars our ponies.

"It's a real beauty. A friend of mine was going in the service and he sold it to me for a steal," he bragged. His pony was a 2012 silver Jeep. "It's got a standard transmission so when I teach you to drive in a few years, you'll have to learn how to shift gears. None of that easy automatic stuff for us."

Great. Another challenge but that's at least three years off. My challenge now is to solve the mystery of the necklace.

We arrived at Bruce's apartment about eight o'clock. He ordered a pizza and we watched one of his favorite movies, *Hands of Steel*, starring Bruce Lee. Then we turned in because we'd be up early the next morning for the powwow.

* * *

"Hey, sleepyhead, wake up." My foot was sticking out from under the blanket and Bruce nudged it with his hand that next morning. I'd spent the night on his couch.

"Rise and shine. Here, I made your cocoa exactly the way you like it," he added holding the steaming mug out in front of me.

"You even remembered the chocolate shavings and little marshmallows," I was so happy he remembered that I almost sang out the words.

"You bet, probably because I like it that way myself. With all your running you can afford the calories. I've had to switch to coffee myself."

Laughter laced his voice. Bruce always had a girlfriend but he didn't like to work out. I guess that was the reason he had started to cut back on sweets.

"I've showered so you're up next, then we can head out to the powwow. Well, after we make a stop," he added.

"A girl?"

"Of course a girl. I want you to meet Lila."

We picked up Lila at her apartment. She was one of those people you like right away and she hugged me after Bruce introduced us. She was as tall as Bruce and her dark brown hair flowed down to her waist. The silver buttons of her white blouse glistened and ropes of turquoise and orange beads circled her neck. She wore earrings of delicate turquoise beads. Two slender silver bracelets were on her left wrist and on her right wrist, she wore a wide silver cuff set with turquoise stones of various sizes. The hem of her denim skirt touched the top of her ankle boots. And even though she wore sunglasses, I knew her eyes would be shining and happy.

"Just so you know, I'm Ojibway. And I'm rocking it old style today," she laughed.

"That means she's wearing a long skirt," Bruce said.

He drove the three of us to the outdoor grounds where the powwow was set up. We bought our passes and then found seats in the area surrounding the arena. The dance area was in the center of the arena. Outside the arena area were the booths where sellers offered food and craft work.

"Here's the plan, ladies. We can sit here for the Grand Entry and then we'll walk around," Bruce explained.

We'd only been in our seats for about 10 minutes when the Master of Ceremonies announced the Grand Entry. He introduced the head male dancer, the head female dancer, the host drum group and the guest drum group. The military veterans entered the arena followed by an honors dance. I sat with Bruce and Lila for about an hour until I became restless. The leather bag holding the necklace rubbed against my chest.

"Is it okay with you two if I take off for a while? I'd like to check out the vendor tables."

"I know you, Cady. You want to check out the fry bread and Indian tacos. But I'm warning you, they won't be as good as mine."

"Your brother makes the best Indian tacos in the world," Lila said. Her mouth was quirking up at the corners as she slipped her arm through his.

"You bet," I agreed and thought I'd give these two some time to be alone.

"Cady, hold up." Bruce used that tone of voice that meant "I love you but there are some rules to be followed here."

"Bruce?"

"Let's meet up in two hours over by that lemonade stand. Two hours, remember, or I'll send the search party out." He sounded like he was kidding but I knew he meant business. He was like our dad in that way.

"Okay, in two hours by the lemonade stand."

The air was warm and the sun was bright. Small children were running around and yelling. I joined the crowd and started walking the outside perimeter of the arena. The aroma of meat cooking over charcoal grills was tantalizing. There were blanket dogs, venison stew and corn soup, fry bread and Indian tacos, baked beans, slushies, soda, ice cream bars, and popsicles. I knew that somewhere there would be a stand selling chocolate cake and banana bread. And coffee, there was always gallons of coffee at powwows.

A man about my grandma's age yelled out his coffee order, "And make it with two sugars and cream." *That's how my dad drinks it. And John Ray!* That little memory warmed me inside. I kept on walking and told myself I'd come back later to buy a small package of wild rice and maybe some maple syrup to take home.

I left the food area and headed for where the craft vendors had set up their tables. The vendors were selling beaded moccasins and pouches, baskets and quill work, dream-catchers, silver and turquoise jewelry, and paintings done in oil and water colors.

I stopped at one table to admire a pair of beaded earrings. They were different from the usual dream-catcher ones and had a matching medallion on a beaded chain-like necklace. Dream-catchers resemble a spider's web and are what we hang over our beds to catch our bad dreams. Then, later, once those bad dreams are trapped in the web, we take the dream-catcher out into the sunlight to have them float away. I didn't have the $200 to buy the earrings but I thought that maybe, with practice, I could copy them. I'd ask my culture teacher if she could help me.

"Would you like to try these on?" The woman sitting at the table held them out to me.

"I would but I can't afford them," I told her.

"I like to call these beads 'little mysteries on thread'," she told me and laughed. Her work was exquisite, painstakingly done. Yellows, reds, blues and white. Each of the colors seemed to flow into the next.

"You're really good at this. You must use really tiny beads. I still use the larger beads."

"Keep practicing and you'll get better. That's the only way, practice. I haven't seen you on the powwow circuit before. Are you from around here?"

"No, I'm from Michigan," I told her.

"*Ahau*," she greeted me and held out her hand for me to shake it. I've always liked the way that word sounds as it rolls around on the tongue of a native speaker.

"Welcome to our powwow. You're not a buying customer but you seem like a good girl. Would you like a soda? I've got a cooler here full to the brim with ice and soda. Maybe a root beer?"

I didn't want to offend her by turning down her offer and I was thirsty. The sun was hot in the arena.

She grabbed a root beer from her cooler, opened it and held it out to me.

"Is something bothering you? Maybe I could help."

I opened my jacket to reveal the leather pouch hanging around my neck. I removed the necklace and held it out to her.

"I'm trying to find out the history behind this necklace," I told her. The little bear seemed to dance in my hand as I held it in the sunlight. The pieces of turquoise and cobalt blue stone were veined with copper, something that showed up in the glare of the sun.

"No, I can't say that I know anything about that necklace, but I know someone who can." She pointed to a row of vendor tables. "Walk down about five booths and then turn left past the T-shirt table. You'll pass another table where they're selling posters and books. Keep going and at the end is an older lady selling some pawn jewelry. I think she might be able to help you. She's quite an expert on the older beadwork."

After I thanked her I had to hold myself back from running to where I hoped to find the older lady. T-shirts, check; posters and books, check; old lady selling pawn...no, she wasn't there. There was only a young boy sitting at a nearby table drinking a slushie.

"Where's the lady selling the pawn jewelry?" I really needed to find her.

"She's gone. She got a phone call a while ago and had to leave." The bright-blue slushie juice ran down his chin and dripped over his hands.

I put the necklace back in the pouch and hung it around my neck once again. I'd been so close. This was frustrating and I was starting to get mad. Would I ever find out the story behind this necklace?

Chapter 11
Waabigwan (Flower)

~~~~~~~~~

Our culture teacher had assigned us a beadwork project a month ago but I hadn't finished it yet. I only had 10 more days before the spring awards banquet when our projects were due.

"Now, class, this project will determine your quarter grade, which is important because it affects your semester grade. And that semester grade will tell me who passes and who doesn't," Iris announced. "And, you know, I don't make exceptions." She took a sip of her Coke and raised her other hand in the air.

"It will be nice for your family to see what you do here in school. I'm going to display your work and I'm throwing in a few surprises. Any questions?"

Kids asked if a beaded keychain would count? A beaded pen? A beaded drumstick? What about earrings and medallions? Disposable cigarette lighter covers? Or did it have to be something bigger? Maybe dance regalia?

"All of those will be fine, but they must be finished by my deadline. Got it?"

I found the design I'd copied from the beadwork table at Bruce's powwow. It was an older pattern, maybe even 100 years old. I sketched a copy of it in my journal and then colored it. The background was white, which meant I'd need a lot of white beads to fill in the space around the design. The main design was of a red rose. A large leaf grew from either side of the flower's stem and each was as long as the stem. Together they resembled the wings on a butterfly. When you viewed the whole design you did a double take. Were you looking at a butterfly or at the flowers's leaves?

I decided to use the same colors I'd seen in the original. Each leaf was divided into four sections with the biggest part at the bottom and the smallest part at the top. There was a line, probably part of the stem, going down the center of the leaf and splitting it. One half was in pale green and the other half was a darker bluish green.

My plan was to transfer my sketch to a piece of graph paper. I'd follow this pattern when doing the actual beadwork using my small loom. I had a good supply of needles. I would need the larger sized beads. When I finished it I'd sew the beadwork onto a piece of backing and then I hoped to sew it onto a small leather bag. When I got to that stage, I'd probably use the thimble my mother had left behind. Grandma had given it to her hoping she'd learn to bead but she never did.

That night I showed the design to my dad.

"This is going to take a lot of beads, Cady. How are you going to pay for them?"

"Our culture teacher has money in her budget to pay for part of it but we have to contribute. Our class is going to hold some Indian taco sales and other stuff and I'll help," I told him.

"That sounds like a plan. Cady, there's something about this pattern you've sketched that looks familiar. Where did you get the design?"

I told him it was one I'd seen at the powwow in Minneapolis and that the woman at the booth had let me copy it.

"Hmm, hang on a minute," he said.

We'd been sitting at the kitchen table. Dad was drinking a cup of coffee and I'd been finishing off the last of my favorite ginger ale. The ginger ale was warm so I'd added lots of ice. I sat there crunching the ice in my mouth, biting down hard on the cold slivers, while I waited for him.

Meanwhile he'd gotten up and walked into the living room. He'd lifted the tray off a flat-topped trunk we used as a table next to the couch. He knelt on the floor and started to rummage through the trunk's contents.

"Yup, it's where I thought it was. I found it." He waved a book so excitedly that the air seemed to crackle with electricity. "I'd forgotten all about this until you showed me your drawing."

I sat there, stunned.

"Come here, Cady."

I crossed into the living room and bent down next to him.

"Here's a photo of my mom, your Grandma Winnie." He handed me the photo album.

My grandma was much younger in the photo, not much older than me. She held a beaded purse in her lap and her smile stretched from one side of her face to the other. I'd never seen a piece of beadwork like it, not even at powwows. It was an old-fashioned clasp purse and even the handle was beaded. The design was the same as the one I'd chosen, only the colors were different.

"See, Cady? The design, placement and arrangement of the beads look the same. I'm guessing the colors are a match also."

My dad was smiling and he even hugged me.

"Imagine this, my daughter has chosen a beadwork pattern that matches one my own mother made more than fifty years ago. This calls for another cup of coffee!"

He stood and walked into the kitchen so he didn't how stunned I was. A few minutes later, I heard the familiar gurgle of the coffee maker as Dad brewed a fresh pot.

I looked at the photo once again. My grandma wasn't alone in the photo. Another young woman stood in back of her. She wore the necklace, my bear necklace, around her neck. I had to blink my eyes and shake my head to be sure it was the same necklace. I even grabbed Dad's new magnifying glass from his desk. He thought I needed a closer look at the beaded purse, but I was looking at the necklace.

Yes, it was the same necklace. I could see the little bear hanging from its middle. Was I imagining it or did he wink at me?

CHAPTER 12
NOW

~~~~~~~~~~

I had only a few days left to work on my bead project for my culture class and I still didn't know the story behind my necklace. My head was spinning. I didn't have any free time. No time to daydream, watch television or hang out with Irish at the mall. Plus, I still had to help out at home. I was starting to get mad about all of this work and needed to calm down.

Miss Grady, my Indian Lit teacher, had asked my permission to publish my interview with Grandma Eunice in the tribal newspaper. She'd even called Grandma Eunice and asked her the same thing. We both agreed that it could be printed. The editor of the newspaper is one of Grandma Eunice's nieces.

"Listen to this, Cady. 'The young writer really captured Grandma Eunice's personality.' Those aren't my words. I'm quoting a newspaper editor. Good job!"

She then explained to me that the editor didn't change one word of mine when she printed the story. I showed the story to Dad that night before dinner.

"Well, Cady, this is good work. I see they even gave you a byline. That means they printed your name and gave you credit for it."

"Yeah, Dad, I know what a byline is. I'm not a little kid and I'm not stupid," I told him. But I smiled because I knew that deep down, he was really trying to be nice.

Even Francine showed she was proud of me because she offered to make my favorite dinner, pork chops and mashed potatoes, to celebrate. She's not the best cook in the world but it made me happy that she was trying to be nice.

Later that night, I sat on the bed in my room and held the necklace in my hand.

Please, little guy. Tell my your story. Life would be a lot easier if someone would tell me why I found this necklace. Wasn't growing up hard enough without mysteries I had to solve? Weren't these supposed to be the best years of my life?

I was so frustrated I wanted to stuff myself with chips and popcorn and licorice and candy bars. But if I ate all that stuff, I'd need gallons of ginger ale to settle my stomach. I had too much to do and making myself sick wouldn't help.

I threw the necklace down and it landed on my pillow. When I picked it up again, I peered across the room at my small bookshelf. I had my favorite books on the top shelf—*Black Beauty*, *The Black Stallion*, and a boxed set of Nancy Drew mysteries. The books had belonged to my mother and she'd given them to me on my seventh birthday when I was in the second grade.

"These were my favorites when I was a little girl, Cady, and now I want you to have them," she'd told me.

I was happy she'd given me something that meant a lot to her. But it wasn't until I started reading them that I appreciated her gift. I learned a lot about horses and a lot about solving mysteries. I'd never told anybody because my friends aren't readers like I am but I was crazy about Nancy Drew stories.

"But, Mom, what's a mystery?" I'd asked at age seven.

"It's a big puzzle that only you can solve," she'd answered. "Maybe someday you'll have a mystery of your very own to solve."

"You mean like why you named me Cady?"

"No, silly. I named you Cady, which is short for Cadet. I was a Cadet for two years and those were good times for me. So I named you after that."

"Is that like a junior version of the Girl Scouts?" I asked her.

"No, but everyone thinks that. I was a crossing guard, or Cadet, in elementary school. We got to leave school early and wear a sash and walk out and stop cars and help people cross the street." Then she laughed and stubbed out her cigarette.

"Pretty cool. Right, kiddo?"

"Yeah, Mom," I agreed—but secretly I wished I'd been named after something else.

I had grown into my name and I liked how it belonged to me alone. No one else was named Cady. But my mom was no longer around for me to talk to. She'd been sick and had been sent away to a hospital for a long time to recover. At the hospital, she'd met her new husband and once she got better, she decided to live with him and move to California. All this had happened before I was even eight years old so I was glad we'd had those talks about the books. But I still wish she was here for me to talk to about the mystery of this necklace.

I was starting to get used to having Francine around, but she wasn't someone I'd talk to about things like this. She seemed more like a big sister than a mother and I didn't want her blabbing to Dad about it. I wanted something of my own to share with Dad and I didn't want her putting her nose into it. John Ray told me it was up to me to find out why I had found the necklace. Why had it come to me? I thought back to what the principal had told me after I found the eagle feather. He'd told me to watch for a special message or a mystery to solve.

My mind was spinning with so many thoughts. Even though it was spring, evenings were still cool in northern Michigan. I took the trash out two days later and when I stepped from the porch to the ground, my foot landed on a patch of oil that had dripped from my dad's car. I fell hard. When I tried to stand, a sharp pain shot through my left ankle. It was as if little shooting stars of hurt were pressing hard against my ankle. After my third attempt at trying to stand, I called out for help. And to make it even worse, I had dropped the trash bag, which now lay broken. Garbage was scattered everywhere. Wads of paper, meat wrappers, used tissues, it was a mess.

I brushed the tears from my eyes and yelled, "Dad!"

As usual he was in the kitchen refilling his coffee cup. It didn't take him long to leave the kitchen and walk down the steps. He shook his head back and forth before holding out his arm to help me. He pulled me up and as I staggered to my feet, I became dizzy.

"Hold on tight now. It's okay, Cady, I've got you but you've done it this time. Looks like your running days are over for a while. Come on, let's get you get up the steps."

Chapter 13
Ankles

～～～～～～

Dad was really nice to me after I fell. He'd helped me up the steps and into the living room. I sat on the couch and he'd elevated my ankle on some pillows and put ice on it. After the swelling had gone down, he'd wrapped it in a stretchy bandage.

"You'll have to wrap this every day for a while, Cady. Best to do so first thing in the morning before the swelling sets in. You can also keep icing it. Tough luck, kid. Sometimes a sprain can hurt worse than a break. But it should heal up fine if you're careful."

He even made me my favorite raspberry iced tea. He liked to joke that he made it from an old family recipe. Every year his relatives up north picked and dried the fruit from bushes they'd been growing for generations. I'm not sure how he made the tea, but it sure tasted good.

I'd missed two days of school because of my sprained ankle. Francine bought crutches for me at Goodwill so I was able to hop around all weekend. By Monday I was restless and pretty good at using the crutches. As long as I didn't put weight on my ankle, I could maneuver around without too much awkwardness.

"Hey, Cady, welcome back," my friends hollered at me when I hobbled off the school bus.

"Yikes, girl, what happened?" they kept asking.

"Oh, you know, one of those little accidents we serious runners have." I tried to make light of it but not being able to run was not really a joking matter. No way was I going to confess to slipping on the oil when taking out the trash.

"Well, good thing you're back. Big things are happening around here," one after another told me.

I thought their smiles seemed suspiciously like smirks. Were they holding out on me? I mean, what was going on?

The big news was that we were getting a two-day vacation from school starting the next day. Something about repairs to the school's roof and needing to shut off the water and both had to be done as soon as possible.

Of course, everybody was excited. Two unexpected days off from school. When the final bell rang that afternoon, we all cheered. Locker doors slammed and kids practically ran into each other in the hallway they were rushing around so fast.

"Yeah, freedom, freedom, free at last," they hollered. Some even made a high-pitched trilling sound as they ran down the hallway.

I tried to keep up but my sprained ankle and crutches were slowing me down.

"I need to make a plan," I muttered to Irish on the bus ride home.

"Oh, so exciting. What kind of plan? Does it involve a boy?"

"No, it doesn't. Gee, Irish, get a grip." And then I couldn't help it and started giggling.

"Can't John Ray help you with this?"

"I asked him but he told me it was my mystery to solve but he did offer to help me with research sometime."

"Oh, yeah, I bet he did. And you're making it up about the library. Who meets a boy at a library? Boring! But you don't want to share, so there!" She nudged me in the shoulder. But it was a hard nudge and I had an aisle seat.

"Be careful, Irish. I almost fell out of the seat."

"Okay. And it's okay that you won't share 'cause you're injured and can't walk or run or anything because I'll be stuck at home babysitting. Want to come join me?"

"Sure." I really didn't, though. What I wanted to do was visit my grandma and ask her about the photo my dad had shown me. I had asked Dad about it but he said he only showed it to me so that I could see the bead pattern. He didn't know anything about a mysterious necklace.

Chapter 14
Necklace

~~~~~~~~~~

That night I told Dad and Francine that we had the next two days off from school.

"Yeah, we got the robocall this morning. Too bad with the end of the school year coming up," Dad commented.

"So, Cady, any plans to go to Florida or Vegas during this long weekend break?" Francine asked, trying not to laugh.

"No, Francine." I dragged my fork around my plate.

Why are they in such a good mood? It wasn't because of tonight's lame meal. Tater tots and hot dogs.

Francine had cooked dinner, which meant that I could count on ice cream for dessert. That was a good thing. Sometimes, for special occasions, she would make a Twinkie cake. Gross. The first time she'd made it had been for her birthday. I'll never forget it. How could I? She was so proud of herself and all she'd done was slice open a couple of Twinkies and then pile on the Cool Whip like it was some big culinary accomplishment. She'd then topped it off with a maraschino cherry and some candles.

"I would like to take a trip. I'd really like to visit Grandma Winnie. I wish she didn't live so far away."

"Hmm." And then Dad cleared his throat again.

He exchanged one of those married people, we're-in-this-together looks with Francine.

"Cady, you might be in luck. I'm driving up to Minnesota to see about a possible web designing project. I was planning on visiting your grandma on my way home. I could change my route and drop you off there for an overnight visit. But we'd have to clear it with her first. How does that sound?"

"I'd love that." My eyes started to fill with tears of relief.

Grandma can help me. I know she can. She always has.

I hadn't been able to visit Grandma since my dad had married Francine and we had moved to Michigan. And now my dad and I would have our very own road trip.

"Just the two of us, Dad? It will be like the old days."

"Yup, I guess it will be. It might get cold, so bring a warm jacket."

"Yeah, Dad, I know."

He still thinks I'm such a little kid and not almost fourteen. I knew that it gets cold at night in Minnesota during the spring. For this trip I planned to wear my new jeans, a T-shirt and a flannel shirt. I don't like to dress too warmly when riding in the truck but I'd bring along my denim jacket. It had a fleece lining so it'd be warm enough if it got cold. I threw in my hairbrush, my coconut shampoo, and a set of beaded barrettes one of my aunts had made for me into my travel bag. I always packed my sketchbook and some pencils for sketching and journal writing. And my old cell phone because I had loaded my favorite songs on it and because I didn't wear a watch.

We left before 6 a.m. next day, Saturday. After I showered and dressed that morning, I put the leather pouch, with the necklace inside it, around my neck and under my T-shirt. I asked Dad if I could take the photo with us.

"It's the one you showed me that's in the trunk in the living room. The one where Grandma was really young and was with some other woman?"

"I don't see why not. It might be nice for you to spend some time talking about the old days with your grandma. And then you could show her that sketch you made for your beadwork pattern."

"Let's get it out now, Dad, so we don't forget," I pleaded.

"You're so impatient, Cady. Sure, we can get it out now. I'd probably forget about it later and we'd be in the truck halfway to Minnesota when one of us remembered it."

He walked into the living room and opened the trunk and handed it to me.

"Here it is. Now take good care of it; it's the only one we've got."

I placed the photo between two thin sheets of cardboard and put them into my sketchbook for safekeeping. I had lots of questions to ask Grandma Winnie and I was crossing my fingers she could answer them.

We ate a quick breakfast and packed sandwiches, apples, and cookies in a cooler bag for our lunch.

"We'll have to stop for gas along the way and to use the restroom. I can load up on coffee when we do and you can get something to drink." Usually Dad likes to kid around and offer to race me to the truck. But I was still limping a little bit so that didn't happen. Instead he was in dad mode.

"Now take it easy walking to the truck. I know you're in a hurry to see your grandma but don't rush. I don't want you falling down again," he cautioned me.

That early in the morning it was still cold despite the sun starting to come up.

The truck's horn beeped and I limped out to the truck and opened the passenger door. At least I didn't need to use crutches anymore.

"Come on, girl, time's a wasting," Dad told me. "It's foggy this early, Cady, so you spot for deer."

I settled back into the seat and focused on both sides of the road, moving my head back and forth. Spotting for deer meant watching for the unexpected appearance of one of those four-leggeds who might decide to suddenly leap onto the road in front of our truck. My dad usually drives pretty fast, but that day it seemed liked he was driving extra slow. I kept glancing at the speedometer. I couldn't believe it. He was going ten miles above the speed limit and it seemed like we were crawling. Dad saw me looking at the dashboard.

"In a hurry, kiddo? You must really want to see your grandma."

"Uh, sure, Dad," I answered back.

Once Dad had turned the truck onto the main highway, I didn't need to watch for deer any longer. I put my earbuds in and listened to music on my phone. It was an old phone but at least I could load my songs onto it. I dug some gum out of my backpack and chewed and chewed. I even blew a few bubbles. Usually my music was a good distraction but today all I could think about was the photo tucked away in my notebook.

Would my grandma wonder why I was so curious? Did I dare show her the necklace? These questions kept circling around and around in my head. What to do? What to do? I touched the little leather pouch hidden under my T-shirt. Silently, I talked to the necklace and the little bear in its center. *Ok, little guy, help me out. Ok?*

I hoped that when I solved the mystery surrounding the necklace, it would help me learn why I had found it. I wanted to learn more about my heritage and I desperately wanted to know if I had a special mission in life. Was I chosen to find the necklace for a special reason? Everything had changed so much at home and I needed to find something to hold onto that wouldn't change. Last year I had even talked to Dad about taking me winter camping.

"No way, Cady. No way. Maybe at one time I might have done it but not now. End of discussion." He refused to tell me why. "My word is final. Go do your homework or see if Francine

74

needs help with anything," he added before leaving me alone in the living room. I heard him rattling around in the kitchen.

"Who took my coffee?" he yelled.

I remembered how frustrated I was when he said that. Bruce had been put out to fast, so why couldn't I? Did someone somewhere somehow hear about this and give me this mystery to solve instead? My shoulders shook when I thought about it like that.

"Stop cracking your gum, Cady, it's giving me a headache. We're almost there, so spit it out." Dad's comments broke into my daydreams.

We pulled up to Grandma's house in time for supper. We'd left eight hours ago and made two rest stops. We hadn't talked to each other during the drive. I listened to my music and Dad listened to his old-time country western songs on the truck's CD player. He liked some old guy named Tom T. Hall. Some of them I liked and some I didn't. It wasn't a bad way to spend a day but I was happy when we got to my grandma's. And I was doubly happy I had my own music to listen to.

CHAPTER 15
WE ARE HUNGRY

"It's about time you two showed up. Come on in, you're here in time for supper," Grandma Winnie said and opened her arms for a hug. "Cady, why are you limping? At least you're still in one piece, so I'm grateful for that."

"Yes, Mom, we all are," Dad added.

What? Did Dad wink at me? And he's calling his mother "Mom." This was different but different in a nice way. I liked it.

Grandma had been cooking all day. She served us a dinner of chili, fry bread and molasses ginger cookies with icing for dessert.

"Mom, your cooking is as good as I remembered. Now I'll top off my thermos with some of that coffee and then be on my way."

Grandma waved her hand.

"On with you, then. Son, your daughter and I have lots to talk about."

After Dad left, Grandma fixed me with one of her stares. She laughed and I noticed she'd lost one of her back teeth. I must have been staring pretty hard at her because she suddenly reached out and touched the tip of my nose with her finger.

"Don't worry about my missing tooth. The dentist at the Indian Health Center promised to fix it up for me as good as new. Your Auntie Ethel is taking me to see him next week. But now we've got more important things to discuss.

"My woman's intuition is telling me that something is bothering you and I want to help. You're only here one night,

Cady, so tell me. What's troubling you? And don't deny it. I've known you since you were a little baby and I can tell when something is bothering you."

I hemmed and hawed because I didn't know where to begin.

Darn it, why did my grandma always have to be so blunt? Why couldn't she take her time and circle around things? Why couldn't we talk about her latest new recipe or ask if I had a boyfriend or even how things were going at home.

I took a deep breath.

I told her about John Ray and interviewing Grandma Eunice and my new bead project. I unbuttoned the top two buttons of my shirt and pulled out the small leather pouch holding the necklace. I took it out and handed it to her.

"I found this necklace hidden in my closet. It looks like the one I saw in a book at the library and Dad gave me the same photo. Look, it's a picture of you and the woman standing next to you is wearing my necklace. I can't figure out why the necklace was hidden and why I found it. The only clue I have is this photo. Do you think it's a sort of quest for me?"

I got up and walked into the living room where I had dropped my backpack. I unzipped it and pulled out my notebook with the photo.

"See what I mean?" I placed the photo on the kitchen table.

"I want to know why I found the necklace and what the photo means. Who's wearing it? Is there a secret story? When I interviewed John Ray's grandma, everything was going really well until a photo fell out. When I reached over to pick it up from the floor, she grabbed it from me and told me to leave. She'd been really friendly up until then. I thought she'd be mean and all that but she was really nice until then. When I talked to John Ray about it, he said he didn't know what I was talking about."

"Why do you want to know about it?" Grandma asked.

"John Ray told me I found it because it's my mystery to solve."

"Some things, Cady, are best left untouched. They're better left in the past," Grandma replied.

"Why won't anyone help me?" I didn't mean to but I was almost yelling. I picked up the photo and grabbed the necklace. "You can see that they match. The woman in the photo is wearing the necklace and you're standing next to her. You know about this, I know you do. Why won't you help me? Why won't you tell me what's going on? I'm almost fourteen and I'm not a little kid anymore even though everyone treats me like one."

And now I was really yelling. I couldn't help it and I started to cry.

Grandma was holding out her arms to me and I flew into them. I was too big to sit on her lap like I did when I was little, but it still was a comfort to have her arms around me. We stayed like that for what seemed like forever but was only a few minutes.

"Go to bed now and we'll talk in the morning. You're too tired to learn of these things tonight."

When I got up the next morning, Grandma was sitting at her kitchen table drinking a cup of coffee. It was one of those old-fashioned kind of tables with chrome legs and a yellow formica top and a drawer for knives and forks.

"There's a fresh pot of oatmeal on the stove. And I've got brown sugar and dried cherries here on the table. The cherries are from that little orchard out back."

Even though I was still upset, I was hungry. I knew she'd gotten up early to make breakfast for me and that the food would hold a lot of love in it. Grandma cooked that way. We believed that the emotions you put into the food you prepared would stay there. I was glad she put love into this food and not anger or envy or hatred or resentment.

And now I believed that way too. Since we'd moved to Michigan, Dad had started to teach me to cook. That's why I had to spend one night a week helping him make dinner. He taught me that if I was feeling down or in a bad mood to think of something happy like my little brother and the way he laughed and threw his cereal all over the kitchen.

"Then put those happy feelings into the food. You don't want any nasty feelings and emotions in there." I tried it and it worked. Sometimes I even played powwow music on the old CD player in our kitchen. I liked Black Lodge and Dad liked to play the old Buffy Sainte Marie stuff.

I fixed myself a bowl of oatmeal and added the brown sugar and cherries. I wanted to apologize but didn't know how. I hoped she'd see that I was trying to make up for my outburst last night.

Grandma held her coffee mug and took a sip and then put the mug back down on the table.

"I did a lot of thinking after you went to sleep last night. You're right about not being a little girl any more. You're almost 14. I wasn't much older than you are when I got married and started a family. Times have changed but some things haven't. One of the things that needs to change is all the secret-keeping around here. That necklace and photo are part of the secret."

I sat there and stared at my oatmeal. I started to pick up my glass of orange juice but couldn't move my arm.

"Cady, are you listening to me? Are you hearing my words?"

"Yes. Please, Grandma, what is all this about?"

"You'll know soon. Eat up and then we'll go outside for a walk and I'll tell you."

Chapter 16
Women

~~~~~~~~~~~~

Grandma's little house was about an hour's drive north of Minneapolis and in the woods. Grandma always claimed she was a country girl and not city folk. My grandpa had built their first and only house before my dad was born. Grandpa died when I was only a baby but Grandma still lived there.

"I like being near the woods, Cady. It refreshes me. The trees seem to know what I'm thinking and feeling and they always comfort me when I'm down. Come on, there's something I want to show you."

I followed her along a narrow path for about a quarter of a mile. The sun was shining brightly when we'd walked across Grandma's backyard but here in the woods its light was filtered softly through the leaves. The path was damp but I didn't mind too much. A few squirrels darted here and there and then I caught sight of it—a blue jay. It was squawking and flying from branch to branch.

"Someone's got a new friend. Or maybe that blue jay is your spirit guide."

"Stop joking, Grandma," I replied. I told her how a blue jay seemed to follow me around a lot and that it always wanted me to look at it.

"He turns up when I don't expect it, like when I'm out running and need to figure things out. I was in a coffee shop with a friend and they even had a bird clock. When it was time for me to leave, the blue jay was the bird chirping the hour. It's crazy and I don't get it."

"The blue jay does seem to favor you, but then blue jays always have ever since you were a baby. There was always one around you somehow. That crazy bird was either jabbering away on a branch outside your bedroom window or watching over you when you played outside. There's nothing wrong with that. Realize it, accept it and learn to work with the messages that little bird brings to you. But that's not what I brought you here to talk about. Sit down over there."

She pointed to a flat rock about the size of a very large cushion. There was another larger rock across from it where she was perched. I sat down crosslegged on the rock and watched her. She lifted her hands from her lap and circled them in the air.

"I have important things to tell you and I need you to focus and to listen carefully. But first I need to put some tobacco down and thank Mother Earth for the gift of this beautiful morning." She took a tiny wooden box, only about an inch and a half square, from her skirt pocket, slid the lid back and shook a bit of loose tobacco into her left hand. She then moved the tobacco into her right hand and carefully shook it onto the ground.

"There, our own little ceremony. It's best to do this at dusk when the spirits are about but you'll be on your way home by then." She picked her eyeglasses up from next to her and put them back to rest on her nose. Grandma once told me that it was important to have your eyes uncovered when making an offering so the Creator could recognize you.

"This story began years ago when I wasn't much older than you are now. I had a few close friends at that time and one of them was your friend John Ray's grandmother, Eunice. She was the best storyteller and singer in our group and she had a beautiful twin sister, Irene.

"Irene, well, she was something. She could dance. She was always the best dancer at the powwows. And she danced all the non-native dances as well. She had a natural rhythm. She used to say that she was born to dance and that must have been true because she lived to dance. The rest of us walked; she glided. She spun and flowed. When she danced it was magic. Her shawl became the wings of a butterfly and she soared through the air.

"Things started to change the summer we were seventeen. There were four of us in our group and we shared the month of June as our birthday month. Oh, we thought we knew everything. We thought we were grown-up women who would take life by the horns and make it do what we wanted. We were young and strong and very confident.

"Our parents had raised us well. They had given us the best of everything they could provide. We never lacked for a warm bed or a roof over our heads. Our bellies were full of good food. We had been educated in the Western way. We spoke our Indian language at home but, unlike our parents, we could speak English and we could read it and write it. We knew how to keep a proper home, how to cook and put food aside for the winter months so it wouldn't spoil and we would have it to eat when the cold weather came.

"Three of us knew how to kill a deer and then how to dress it. How to hang it upside down from a tree branch so the blood drained out and then how to butcher it. We could sew and quilt. I was known throughout Indian country for my beadwork and Irene was known for her dancing. Life was good and we laughed and sang through our days.

"The bad time came when Irene started to have dreams. She didn't tell us this was happening but we knew that something was upsetting her. She still danced and laughed but we knew that she was changing. And, then, one day, all four of us were together. It was a hot afternoon in late July. We had each finished our chores and had met for a picnic near this very spot where we are sitting now.

"We'd laid out our lunch. Eunice had made egg and onion sandwiches and I'd brought some venison jerky. We had picked blueberries and raspberries and Yvonne, the other one in our group, had made sun tea. It was very hot, so hot the mosquitoes had stopped their buzzing and the flies were leaving us alone. Even the ants were taking a nap. Yvonne and I decided to go wading in that stream you see over there. Eunice and Irene wanted to nap.

"Yvonne and I were splashing each other and cooling off. That water was so refreshing on such a hot day and we had waded in up to our knees. But then a scream cut through the air. We rushed back up here and found Eunice and Irene shaking and crying.

Grandma pulled a handkerchief from her pocket and wiped her eyes.

"Even these memories can still make me cry," she whispered. I stood and moved closer to her. Bending down, I asked, "What happened then? Tell me, tell me." It was hard to breathe I was so caught up in Grandma's story. I clutched the little bag I wore around my neck, feeling the necklace inside.

"Irene was crying so hard she couldn't talk so Eunice spoke for both of them. She had fallen asleep and dreamed that Irene was taken away from us. 'Something dark came down on her and suddenly she was gone,' Eunice told us."

Grandma looked at me.

"Keep going, Grandma please,"

"Irene then wiped her eyes on the sleeve of her dress and said, 'I'm frightened because I've had that same dream three times and now my twin had it. Soon everything will change.'

"We were upset and wanted to know what the dream meant. Yvonne begged Irene to tell us but all she would say was, 'You know what it means.' And then Irene stood up and walked away from us until we could no longer see her. That broke up our good mood. We packed up our things, rolled up our blankets, and walked home. And, soon, everything did change. We tried to pretend that it hadn't but we knew it had.

"I got a job in town that fall. I was able to live at home and when the weather was nice, I walked or rode my bike. My friend, Ben, drove the school bus and he'd give me a ride during the bad weather. I was glad I could help my folks out with their expenses and I liked getting out and meeting new people.

"Yvonne went to North Dakota to train as a nurse. She had people up there who she stayed with. She was good about staying in touch and wrote to me almost every week. But with Irene and Eunice, things were different. They quit visiting me. If I wanted to see them, I had to go to their place and they were gone a lot. To this day I don't know where they'd go or what they did to pass the time.

"That next summer, we learned that Eunice had married John Ray's grandfather and moved to his reservation in Michigan. Their families were close and the two of them had met up at a powwow and had fallen in love. Irene stayed with her parents but after a few months, she wanted to move to be near her twin. She missed her too much. She found a job as a seamstress at a large furniture factory near Eunice's place. She was a fine seamstress so they were happy to hire her to do their sewing.

"She moved in with some distant cousins. They lived in town and rented half of a house. Each half had an upstairs and a downstairs. Irene got along well with her cousins. They were an older couple whose kids were grown and then they had a surprise baby late in life. Having Irene there to help watch the baby made them real happy. Irene didn't really like town life but was able to meet up with her sister almost every weekend. Eventually, Eunice started having babies of her own and the two sisters weren't able to visit with each other as much.

"After that, Irene had more time on her hands, especially on weekends. Well, at least until George moved in next door to her. Oh, Cady, he was a handsome fellow not much older than Irene. He made his living working in the woods cutting brush and selling it, but he wanted more out of life. He wanted to buy a place of his own and maybe a car so when he was offered a job at the furniture factory, he didn't think twice about taking it. He was skilled with all those tools and could fix almost anything. It wasn't long before he was promoted to foreman.

"He and Irene took a liking to each other and soon they were walking to work together. If the weather was too cold, they'd catch a ride with Irene's cousin or ride the bus."

"Did they fall in love, Grandma?"

"Of course they did. Soon they were going to powwows on the weekends and Irene was dancing again. She was so happy and I'm guessing George was too."

"But, Grandma, what about the dream?"

"I'm getting to that, Cady. Let me finish. At one of those powwows, an old woman approached Irene and said she had to talk to her. 'You are the one I've been looking for. Come with me.' They went into the old lady's tent where she'd set up a camp for the weekend. She told Irene things that would happen in her future and gave her the necklace."

"You mean the necklace I found?"

"Yes, Cady, I'm certain it's the same necklace. Irene was living with her cousin in the house where you and your family are now living. I think she had a premonition before she hid it in the closet."

"Grandma, are you saying that Irene was chosen by someone from the spirit world to wear the necklace?"

"Yes, Cady. And now you've been chosen to wear it."

"But, why?

"You've got to figure that out for yourself."

When Grandma made up her mind about something, she stuck to it. She liked to say that she was stubborn as paper stuck to duct tape. My dad was the same way and so was I. I knew I wouldn't get any more information out of her during this visit.

A few minutes later, we were walking through her backyard when the tires of my dad's truck crunched on the gravel outside her house.

"It's been fun having you here, Cady." She pulled me into her chest with a tight hug.

I knew she loved me and part of me hated to leave but I was thankful for the time I had spent with her during this visit.

"We'll see each other soon. Right?"

"Sooner than you think, Cady. You start watching for me. I'll be sending my messenger."

Then she turned to my dad. His truck was parked a few feet away. He'd walked up to us so quietly I hadn't heard him.

"You know what I'm talking about. Don't you, son?"

"Of course, but I thought you were done with that stuff," he replied.

"You know better than that. Just because you've walked away doesn't mean our family will ever be done with it." She turned on her heel and winked at me.

"Another puzzle for you, Cady. Now watch out for blue jays." And with a brief wave of her hand she walked up her driveway.

Great, another mystery to solve. Was she referring to the moccasin telegraph? It was amazing how fast information, even gossip, was passed from one Indian family to another—even across state lines. Or was she referring to Dad's earlier training as a medicine man? Could he sense when people would visit? Maybe this was why the blue jay followed me. That crazy bird did help me figure things out in my own head. It tried to warn me when I wanted to do something stupid by distracting me.

And with that she moved away, grabbed a brown paper sack and handed it to him.

"Here, I've packed you some sandwiches for your trip home. And, Cady, I put a little something extra in your duffel bag but don't open it until you're home. Promise?"

"So, you had a good visit with Grandma?" We'd left the back roads and were now in Dad's truck driving down the highway. His question was more of a comment.

"Yes," I answered.

"Good."

He then switched on the radio and listened to the first station he found. The announcer was talking about the weather and how it would affect farm crops. Twenty minutes later the music started. It was Dad's favorite, old-time country and western. I listened for a while and then pulled out my old cell phone and plugged in my ear buds. I was glad I could play my own music and tune out the rest of the world.

We stopped about four hours later to gas up the truck and use the station's restrooms. Dad bought coffee for himself and a root beer for me. We ate Grandma's sandwiches. She'd packed tuna fish and egg salad and a half dozen of her homemade peanut butter cookies. It took another three hours to reach home.

Later that night when I was alone in my room, I unpacked my duffle bag and found the small present Grandma had given me. The package fit easily in my hand and was wrapped in heavy brown paper. Something was causing a bulge in the middle so that the wrapping paper didn't lay flat. I unwrapped it carefully.

My mind refused to accept what my eyes were viewing. How did Grandma know? Nestled into a small piece of cotton wadding were two earrings. Tiny turquoise beads had been stitched to a leather backing. Miniature white bears, carved from stone and no bigger than the thumbnail on my pinkie finger, hung from each turquoise circle. They were a perfect match to my necklace.

I reached for the brown paper wrapping to flatten it out. It was then I found the note Grandma had written. She sent me a birthday card and Christmas card each year and always added a few sentences telling me about what she was cooking or where she'd made a new path for walking. I knew her handwriting.

"Cady, this is the next part of your journey. This mystery is yours to solve. I know you will solve it. Be patient and watch for the signs."

CHAPTER 17
EARS

~~~~~~~~~~~~~~~~~

I wanted to cry, but I didn't. Part of me was happy because Grandma now knew that I had found the necklace. Irene had been chosen to wear it by the spirit world for her strength and her dancing. But why had I been chosen?

I was proud that Grandma had shared Irene's story but I was scared because I didn't know what I had stumbled into. Why couldn't I just find the answers on the Internet or from asking an elder? I would tie a hundred prayer ties and make tobacco offerings every day for a month if an elder would just tell me the reason I'd found the necklace. The old me would have thrown something against the wall or slammed a drawer. I would have made a lot of racket because I was frustrated. The new me sat on my bed and held the earrings in my hand. I put the necklace next to them.

What is going on here? What is this all about?

The earrings had another special meaning. My dad had once told me that when a young traditional Indian girl has her first moon time, it is marked with a ceremony. It recognizes this time of change when a young girl becomes a woman. Gifts and a new name, an Indian name that the spirits will recognize her by, are given to the girl. Dad promised me that I would have my ears pierced for the ceremony. He would then give me my first pair of pierced earrings.

But that all changed after he married Francine. She had grabbed me one Saturday afternoon a few short weeks after she moved in with us. She was bored in our small house and with waiting for her baby to be born.

She threw my jacket at me and said, "Come on. We're going to the mall. Your dad's got an appointment and he won't even know we're gone."

Sometimes Francine's words sound like a little girl's and although she's 24 years old, she is my stepmother. So, I have to do what she tells me to do. She picked up the car keys and unlocked Dad's desk drawer. She slipped two $20 bills from a bank envelope into her purse and locked the drawer again before putting the keys back in her pocket.

"It's time you had your ears pierced," she told me.

"But won't Dad be mad? The family rule is that I have to wait until my naming ceremony. And shouldn't Grandma be there when I have it done?"

My voice was soft like a whisper because I was so surprised.

"Forget about that because we're changing things around here. Come on. I want to do something nice for you and it will be fun," she said in that odd little-girl voice of hers.

We'd gone to the little boutique at the mall where Francine talked to the lady who worked there. She was wearing a white jacket with her name, Janice, pinned to it.

"Can you use that special staple gun to pierce my stepdaughter's ears?"

"Of course. And there's no charge if you buy some earrings," the lady told Francine.

I had to sit on a high stool and hold really still. She put that stapler up against my ear lobes one at a time and pierced them. It stung. A lot. No one told me about that part but I was still excited. I had to wear a small, dark gray ball in each ear lobe for two weeks afterwards.

"Trainers, I call them," explained the lady who sold them to us.

She then told me to wash the sore spots on each ear lobe with alcohol and cotton balls. I did that every morning and every night for three weeks and I never forgot. Irish had her ears pierced last year and forgot to keep them clean afterwards and she got a huge infection. I didn't want that to happen to me so I added an extra week to the two weeks the lady at the mall had told me about.

I was surprised that Dad wasn't mad about what we'd done. Francine showed him my newly pierced ears and he shrugged his shoulders.

"It's okay as long as you're happy, Cady," was all he said.

I couldn't believe it. There had been a time he would have called down the thunder gods on us for what we'd done. Now he shrugged his shoulders and walked away. But he never mentioned my naming ceremony again. I hated them both for that. Now there would be no naming ceremony for me—no feast surrounded by family and friends who loved me, no gifts, and no special name. How would I know what my future path would be? I had cherished the dream of this special day for so long and now it was gone. I had been duped. Grandma knew how important that ceremony would have been to me, another reason these earrings were such a special gift.

Just then there was a tapping on my window. I glanced up and there was that blue jay again.

Tap, tap, went his beak against the glass of the window. Tap, tap. I walked over to the window and raised it. The bird flew to a nearby branch where it perched. It cocked its head in my direction and made that funny bird sound, *toolool, toolool*. The second time he made that blue jay noise, it sounded like words.

"Don't be sad, don't be sad. I'm here." And with that it flew off.

Chapter 18
Noongom (Today)

My ankle had healed so I could run and I was feeling better. And I was still trying to solve the mystery of the photograph. And now we only had a few days left before the end of the school year. I hadn't finished my beadwork project and I had final exams to study for. I figured once I knew more about that photo, I'd know more about why I had found the necklace and what it meant for me. Even though Grandma had told me about her friend, Irene, and the others in the photo, I was still puzzled. Why had Grandma Eunice been so upset when I saw the photo at her house?

Darn, I should have asked Grandma about that and who knows when I'll see her again.

I couldn't call her and ask her on the phone because she didn't like to tell me about things that way.

"Cady, some of the things I teach you are spiritual and you know we only talk about those things person to person and not on the phone. That's not our way."

John Ray talked to me at school and sometimes he'd even sit with me at lunch but I never saw him outside of school. He was training for a boxing tournament at the end of June.

"You know I like you, Cady, but I like boxing too. This is my big chance and I need to train. Coach hounds me all the time and said I should forget about socializing for the next month and I'm going to do that. After the tournament, I'll have more time. Besides, you've got that mystery to solve."

Yeah, I did, but part of me thought maybe he was trying to brush me off.

I didn't even see Irish as much as I wanted to. Her mom needed her to babysit and Irish, being Irish, had another new boyfriend.

"It's kind of like that guy Forest Gump says in the movie, Cady, 'Life is like a box of chocolates.' It's that way with boys, there are a lot of them and each one is different. They're fun but you know me. I get bored really quick and like to move on."

Because my phone was older, texting didn't always work too well. I liked it better when she called. The first time Irish called me after my visit to Grandma's, I could hear the excitement in her voice. Irish hated to text; she always called. She had too much energy to text, and couldn't stay still long enough.

"Cady, can you meet me at the mall? Mom won at Bingo last night and she shared her winnings with me. Come on, it will be fun. I'm buying new clothes and I'll buy us lunch at McDonald's. I'm here now. Meet me in five minutes?"

Irish had told me many times how proud she was of her mom for giving up drinking and partying. "Now Bingo is her way of socializing and relaxing and that's a good thing." And she turned out to be pretty lucky at it. So lucky that Irish didn't mind babysitting for her if it meant she'd be paid and later could go shopping at the mall.

"Irish, even if I ran my fastest, I'd never get to the mall in five minutes," I told her.

"No problem. My mom will give you a ride. She'll pick you up in 10 minutes." Then she hung up the phone.

I pulled on my favorite faded jeans and a new T-shirt my brother had bought me at the powwow. I'd managed to save about $10 and stuffed the bills in the pocket of my jeans. But before I left, I wanted to see the necklace. I had hidden the earrings under my pillow and now I placed those next to the necklace's leather pouch in its hiding place in the closet. I had to move the pouch a bit to make room for the earrings in their wrapping. It was then I noticed a piece of newspaper sticking up.

I left the closet and rummaged around in the top drawer of my bureau where I found my tweezers. I went back to the closet, knelt down and very carefully pulled out the torn piece of newspaper. At the top was a date, February 12, 1956. Only a few lines of type remained, but the first line was intact.

The beautiful Irene, dancing tonight at the auditorium.

I put the small piece of newsprint in an old envelope and stuffed it in my jeans pocket. *Great,* I thought, *now I've got more clues to add to the ones I've already have. Just what I don't need.* But negative thinking wouldn't help me solve the puzzle.

I was standing under the big oak tree in our front lawn waiting for Irish's mom when I heard the familiar racket of the blue jay. That bird kept chattering but this time his noise didn't distract me. It made me think in new ways.

Maybe the earrings were the next step in solving this mystery. If I could find the original newspaper article then maybe I could solve the mystery of the necklace.

Our Social Studies teacher had once told us that microfilm copies of old newspapers were kept at the public library. A few minutes later, I was jostled out of my daydreaming by the beeping of a car's horn. Irish's mom had driven up while I'd been watching the blue jay. She rolled the window down and waved at me.

"Come on, girl, get a move on it. Irish is waiting. You can get in the front seat."

She was laughing and chewing gum. A few minutes later, she dropped me off in front of McDonald's. The car was huffing and puffing as she waited for me to get out.

"Have fun, Cady, and keep an eye on Irish for me. She's a handful, that one."

I barely had time to close the car door when she gunned the engine of her old Pontiac and drove off.

It was easy to find Irish in McDonald's even though it was crowded. She was sitting in one of booths and stood up and started pumping her arms in the air to get my attention. I was walking toward her when she ran up to hug me. She then moved both of us up and down in an improvised little dance movement.

"You're here, you're here," she screeched.

"Yes, I'm here," I replied trying my hardest not to laugh. When Irish was in one of her upbeat moods, it was contagious. Her happiness spread to everyone around her like sunshine blessing a patch of flowers.

I pulled back and noticed her new sweater. It was bright green, of course, her favorite color. She was wearing new jeans.

"Wow, those are really tight."

"Yeah, aren't they great?" she replied.

But it was her boots which caught my eye. She was sporting brown leather ankle boots with a chunky four-inch heel. A silver snake seemed to wrap around each heel.

"Awesome clothes, Irish. I like them."

She spun around showing off her new outfit once again. "Yup, so do I," Irish agreed. "Let's eat."

We went to the counter to place our orders. A few minutes later we were sitting in our favorite booth, the one with seats covered in red leather-looking plastic. Our feast was on the table in front of us: one large chocolate milkshake, one large strawberry milkshake, one large cheeseburger with the works, one Big Mac, one large order of chicken McNuggets and two large orders of fries. I'd forgotten to order an apple pie and told myself I'd go back for one later.

"If I keep eating like this, these jeans won't fit. But it tastes so good and it's so good to finally see you and to get out of the house."

"I hear you," I agreed and trying to stifle a yawn at the same time.

"Am I boring you?" She was vigorously chewing her remaining three french fries.

"You never bore me, but I am a little sleepy."

"How's John Ray? He's been your boyfriend for a while now. Good going," she practically shouted, almost knocking over what remained of her milkshake.

My cheeks were warming and I tried not to blush.

"I like him a lot but I don't know if he's my boyfriend. I haven't seen him outside of school since I interviewed Grandma Eunice. And now he's training for a boxing tournament and he told me he can't spend any time with me until that's over."

"Gee, Cady, that's tough. But it won't last forever and there are other guys out there."

"I know, Irish, but none of them are like John Ray. He's special."

"You're a goof, you know that? Don't get so serious. Let's have fun."

"Sure thing." I told myself I'd start having fun once I solved the mystery of the necklace. And that brought my thinking back to the newspaper clipping I'd found. I would show the clipping to that nice lady in the reference section and maybe she could help me find out more about Irene and George.

Chapter 19
Look for Something

On Monday of our last full week of school before the summer vacation, I couldn't wait for classes to end. After the final bell I almost ran to the bus outside the school's front doors. I told the bus driver, Gus, to let me off at the library in town.

"Can't do that, kiddo. I have to drop you off at home. Those are the rules."

"But I really need to so some research there. It's important," I told him.

"Got a cell phone? I know your dad's voice. Call him up and if he says it's okay, I'll do it. That's my best offer."

Dad had given me that old phone so I could listen to my music but he also paid for 30 minutes usage each month. "Those minutes are for emergency use only, Cady. It's not for calling up your friends and jabbering away until all hours of the night. Remember that. Emergencies only," he had told me.

I considered this an emergency. I called Dad at home and put him on speaker mode so Gus could hear.

"I'm proud of you, Cady. Getting into your studies like this is a good thing. Sure, let me talk to the driver."

I handed the phone to Gus. After the two of them talked, he handed the phone back to me.

"Thanks, Gus. It's really important."

Thirty-five minutes later Gus pulled up in front of the library. I was the last student off the bus. He honked the horn and made a big fuss over me.

"Better get to it then, super student." The way he said those words made me laugh.

"Okay, then." I made a thumbs-up sign. I left the bus and heard someone shouting to me.

"Cady, over here. Wait for me."

John Ray waved to me from across the street. He held a brown to-go cup of coffee and was walking on the sidewalk in front of the coffee shop. He crossed the street to join me.

"What's going on? How come you're going to the library and didn't tell me? We could have met for coffee first."

"Because you told me I wouldn't be seeing much of you; you said you had boxing practice. You said you'd be too busy to spend time with me so how come you're here now?"

"Uh, yeah. Coach had to go to a funeral and called off practice for today so I hitched a ride to town and stopped for a coffee."

I was happy to see John Ray and to talk to him but I was a little mad at him. Did he think I was a mind-reader? How was I supposed to know his practice was cancelled?

"Besides, you know I don't like coffee. You keep forgetting that one little thing."

"I get it. Let me finish this and I'll join you." He gulped down the last of his drink. He tossed the cup in the trash bin and reached over to hold the library door open for me.

"Wait a minute, John Ray. There's something I have to tell you before we go inside." I tugged lightly at his jacket. "Let's sit down here while I explain."

I moved to sit on an old wooden bench in front of the library's double doors. John Ray nudged me to move over and sat down next to me.

"Okay, I'm all ears. Spill."

"It's about the necklace. I found this newspaper clipping. But it's only part of a clipping and I need to see the rest. I thought

I might find it in the microfilm files here." I showed him the clipping and the photo, which were both hidden in the sketchbook in my backpack.

"Let me see that necklace."

I reached for the leather thong holding the small pouch around my neck. I loosened it and withdrew the necklace. I gave it to John Ray, who then held it against the photo.

"I think you're on your way to solving the mystery, Cady. This really does seem like the same necklace in the photo." His words were so faint I had to lean in to hear him. "But how come you're just looking at old newspaper files now? Why didn't you do this a long time ago?

"Because I'm stupid. Because I just found the clipping now. Because your grandma and my grandma clam up and won't answer my questions. Because you and Dad and even that stupid bird tell me I have to solve it on my own. I'm no Nancy Drew; I'm just learning how to do this!"

I bent down and picked up a few pieces of loose gravel and threw them against a nearby flower pot. "So there, Mr. Smarty Pants."

"Gee, Cady, relax. Okay? And, who's Nancy Drew? Do I know her?" but he touched me softly on the shoulder with his knuckles.

I took a deep breath to calm myself and then stood and walked into the library. He followed me and within a few minutes he was leading me because he knew exactly where to go. He turned to see why I was lagging behind him.

"Come on, the microfilm is stored in the genealogy room. My grandpa used to drag me in there when I was a kid. He was always researching our family history. That's why I know where to go."

We walked through the room for the little kids and I laughed when I passed the rowboat.

"My grandpa was always pulling me out of that boat," John Ray said. "He'd be in the genealogy room doing his research and I'd run in here and hop in the boat. I'd pretend I was a pirate. It's crazy the stuff little kids think of."

I grinned as I pictured John Ray as a little boy. I followed him into the genealogy room.

"What's the date on that newspaper story?"

I dug the clipping out of my backpack. "February 12, 1956."

He walked up to a row of old-fashioned wooden file cabinets. They were so old their original brown color had turned almost black. The drawers were smaller than those of the metal file cabinets I was used to seeing at school. There was a little metal card holder attached to the front of each drawer. I stepped closer to read one of those cards and realized that they stated the dates of the microfilm in each particular drawer.

"Got it!" John Ray exclaimed as he pulled one of the drawers open. "Let's load it up." We were looking at an old gray metal Minolta machine. He held the roll of microfilm out to me.

"But, John Ray, what is that? What am I supposed to do with it?"

"It's the microfilm you need. It's a spool holding yards and yards of microfilm. I have an uncle who still prints his own photos in his darkroom. And this microfilm looks like the negatives he uses only this microfilm is in a long strip."

"Uh, John Ray, I'm not sure what to do with that," I told him.

"It's not hard once you know what to do. You can watch me." He sat down in front of the old Minolta microfilm reader. "They haven't updated some of the older files to the new system yet. I guess they ran out of money so we'll have to use this old machine."

He took the end of the film and slotted it into a spool, which he then fit over a spoke that was sticking up.

"Got it." He started cranking the roll. "Next I'll get the lights on." He flicked the switch and we could see a page of the newspaper on the machine's screen. Only it was in reverse—white print on a black background and not black print on a white page the way it is in an actual newspaper.

"John Ray, shouldn't it be black type on a white background?" I asked him.

"Cady, we're working with a negative so this is the way it's going to show up." The spool squeaked until John Ray stopped cranking it around and around.

"Aha, I think I've found it. Was there a page number on your clipping?"

"It was page seven. The print was faded but I could still read it."

He cranked the machine's handle until he got to page seven. "Here it is, Cady. Do you want a copy?"

"How do we do that? Yes, I want a copy! I need to read that story." My voice was cracking I was so excited.

"Go find the librarian and tell her we need a copy. Here, I wrote down the newspaper's date and page number. She can print it out for us but we'll probably have to pay for it."

"But I've only got $5 with me," I told him.

"That's okay. I think they charge $2 per page."

"I want to read it now, John Ray. Please, it's important."

"Okay, give me the $2 and I'll go find the librarian. They're closing in 15 minutes so we've got to hurry."

I gave him the money and then sat down in front of the screen. John Ray had shown me how to make the type size bigger so the article was easier to read.

"Oh, my gosh, my gosh, my gosh," I couldn't help saying out loud as I read the story. "Oh, my gosh," I shouted and pounded the table.

Chapter 20
Grease

~~~~~~~~~~

"Cady, I couldn't find the librarian and they're chasing us out of here." If John Ray hadn't touched me on the shoulder, I wouldn't have heard him. It was as if I was in a trance. He waved his hand back and forth in front of my eyes.

"Cady, come on. They're closing. We've got to leave now."

"What?"

"It's time to go. We can come back tomorrow and get a copy of the story then," he added.

"Oh, yeah, right. Tomorrow. But, John Ray, look what I found!" I pointed to the screen.

I finally had the clues I needed. The old newspaper story showed three women: my Grandma Winnie, John Ray's Grandma Eunice and her twin sister, Irene, who would have been John Ray's great-aunt. Underneath the photo was this caption: Trio Takes Home Top Prizes at Powwow.

The story told how the three had won prizes for their singing, dancing, and beadwork at a powwow held earlier that week in Marquette, Michigan. All three were dressed in their traditional regalia. Irene was in the center and held an eagle feather fan in her right hand. All three seemed happy. And next to it was another photo, but someone had blocked out a lot of the story that went with it.

I stood up and pushed the chair back and then bent down to pick up my backpack.

John Ray walked the ten blocks to my house with me. I was hardly limping anymore but it didn't matter because I didn't notice my feet or anything else. He tried talking to me several times but I couldn't concentrate on what he was saying. My head was full of what I had read at the library.

"John Ray, that was amazing! Next to the photo of the three women I found the same photo that my dad gave me but someone had blackened out most of the the print in the story underneath the original. All that was left was one line, "The fabulous Irene says she will dance no more. What to you think that meant?"

I started to walk past my own yard when John Ray grabbed my elbow.

"Cady, slow down. We're here."

"What? Where?" And then I looked away from John Ray and noticed Dad standing in the driveway.

"Come on, I'll introduce you." I motioned for him to follow me.

Dad was watching us as we approached him and once again his face resembled thunder clouds passing across the sky. It's the face he reserves for strangers. But then, suddenly, he broke into a huge smile.

"I don't believe it. You must be Marion's child and all grown up. John Ray, isn't it?" He extended his hand to shake John Ray's.

"Yes, sir. But do we know each other?"

"We sure do. The last time we met you were a little guy, probably in kindergarten. But I'd recognize that face of yours anywhere. You resemble your grandpa," dad replied.

"I've been told that more than once. Nice to see you again, sir. Cady, I'll see you at school tomorrow." He walked back down the driveway and I knew he would soon be out of sight.

"Can I offer you a ride home, son?" dad shouted after him.

"No, sir. It's okay. I'm walking over to my uncle's and I'll catch a ride out to the rez with him."

Dad and I stood there and watched John Ray as he walked down the block and around the corner.

"Nice boy, that one. Comes from a good family. You could do a lot worse, my girl." I think he actually tried not to grin but it didn't work.

"Dad, it's not like that," I told him.

"Hmm." He walked back to the house and up the steps into the kitchen where I followed him.

"I made potato salad earlier this afternoon. You can get that heavy cast-iron skillet out from the cupboard and start heating grease in it for fried chicken," he told me. I was so excited about what I'd found out at the library that I'd forgotten that it was my night to help Dad cook.

"Uh, Dad, could I help you tomorrow night instead?"

"No, Cady. Francine and your little brother are at a mother-baby thing and I told her I'd have dinner ready at 6 o'clock when they get home. Tonight's your night to help."

Okay, okay. I mentally reviewed what I'd learned at the library and kept looking at the clock. Hurry up, hurry up.

I started rummaging around in the cupboard looking for the skillet. I thought about the newspaper article I'd found on the microfilm and wasn't focused on cooking. What did that newspaper story mean? The fabulous Irene would dance no more. I knew who Irene was but why had she stopped dancing? Is that why she'd hidden the necklace?

"So, you and John Ray? Anything special I should know? Seems you two have been getting pretty friendly lately. I recall you interviewed his grandmother."

"We're friends, Dad, friends. Nothing more." But his question made me a little nervous. I liked my personal life to be my own. I didn't even share my most private feelings with Irish, so I certainly didn't want to open up to Dad about how much I loved John Ray.

"Just checking, Cady." He even smiled a little and I was so glad to see it that I almost dropped the skillet. It reassured me that everything was getting better between us. When he added that he'd bought my favorite ice cream, mint chocolate chip, I knew that he was really trying to pay more attention to me. Things had changed since our trip to see Grandma. It was more peaceful between us. I didn't know the reason, but whatever it was, I was glad.

Francine and my baby brother came home a little later and at six o'clock, we sat down to dinner together. I ate four pieces of fried chicken and a big serving of potato salad and Dad made sure my portion had hard-boiled eggs in it. I fixed myself a huge bowl of ice cream for dessert.

"Well, someone was hungry. Go on, I can tell you're bursting to get to your homework. Francine and I will clean up."

But it wasn't my homework I wanted to work on. I had a mystery to solve.

Chapter 21
Ishkwaandem (Door)

~~~~~~~~~~~

Dinner was over and I was finally alone in my bedroom. I didn't want to be interrupted so I put an old brick in front of the bedroom door. Dad or Francine could still push the door open but I'd have time to hide my notes and the necklace. The brick was another thing my mom had left behind. She'd covered it with a piece of needlepoint she'd made. It had a big yellow sunflower design on a green background and even though it was faded, it still seemed as if that flower was smiling at me.

"I designed this when I was pregnant with you, Cady, so it's really special," she once told me. She had even stitched her initials into the bottom corner so we wouldn't forget who had made it.

I like having things around me that my mom has given me. I've stared at that brick more than a hundred times. I've taken it with me whenever we moved. But tonight was the first time that I examined it. It was as if I were studying it. My mom had put a little blue jay in the center of that sunflower. Was that why that bird kept following me wherever I went? Was this her way of telling me she'd always be with me? Deep inside, I hoped this was true. Then I told myself it was time to get to work.

I spread out all the pieces to the mystery of the necklace on my bed. There was the necklace and its leather pouch. There were the two matching earrings, the newspaper clipping, and the photo my dad had found in the trunk. I took my sketch pad and pen from my backpack and sat down on the bed. I wrote down as much as I could remember from what I'd read off the microfilm at the library.

The photo I had was of the same three women in Grandma Eunice's photo but it was a different one. They weren't wearing their regalia; they wore skirts and shirts. And they had pinned their hair up.

"Oh, that," my grandma had explained. "We did that because it was so hot that day. All three of us wanted our hair off our necks. I remember, my hair was so heavy back then. Thick and black and not white like it is today," she'd added laughing.

According to the newspaper story, Irene announced at the powwow that she was giving up dancing.

"Dancing is over for me. I'll never dance again," she told the reporter.

I called Grandma that night after I had asked Dad's permission to do so. He told me to use my phone and that he'd put more minutes on it tomorrow.

"Hi, Grandma, it's me, Cady." I was sitting cross-legged on my bed with the door shut.

"I was wondering how long it would take you to call me. That little friend of yours, the blue jay, came by earlier today. I knew it wouldn't be long before I heard from you."

"Grandma, I don't have a lot of time but I need to talk to you. I went to the library and researched that photo I showed you. I found a story about your friend, Irene. She told everyone she was going to quit dancing. She was famous for her dancing, so why would she do that?"

"Cady, I don't like talking about these things over the phone. You'll have to be patient and wait a while longer to find out. Your uncle is driving me to your school's reservation for an elders' meeting next month. I'll talk to you then, but I've got to go now. Give my love to everyone." Then she hung up the phone.

It was now early June and the temperatures were in the low 70s during the day. Even the flowers seemed happy that winter was over. We had a few red tulips starting to bloom in the backyard and the lilac trees were blossoming.

The spring awards banquet was held over the weekend in one of the large rooms at the casino. I hadn't been on any of the sports teams but my teacher Iris had laid down the law.

"All of my Culture class students must attend—or else." None of us wanted to find out what her "or else" might mean. So Dad went with me. The usual awards were given out for basketball and volleyball. New players on each team were given a school letter jacket with their names embroidered over the front pocket.

And then Iris stood up and announced, "Tonight I am proud to give out awards for accomplishments in our Culture program." She announced the winner for most fluent and most improved in our native tongue.

"And, I am happy to announce the winner for best beadwork." A senior boy won that. I didn't know him or recognize his name so I was daydreaming about the necklace when I heard my name announced.

"Yes, that's right folks, our new addition to class this year, Cady, is this year's Most Improved. She had to struggle with her needle and loom and she's getting there. Her designs are what set her apart. She's a gifted artist and excels at restoring some of our oldest and most traditional designs and bringing them to life."

My prize was a trophy and a $20 gift card to the mini-mart next to the casino. But the best prize was the smile Dad gave me. I'd remember this night for a very long time.

The next day was my 14th birthday. Dad and Francine gave me the new black running pants I wanted. Bruce sent me a silver jacket. It had a hood and lots of zippered pockets. On the front was a small Minnesota patch.

And John Ray? He was still around but totally caught up with his training for the boxing club, which meant he was pretty much out of my life and I missed him. My life had settled down but it was almost too quiet. Until the afternoon when John Ray stopped me in the hall at school.

"Hey, Cady, I know it's kind of late but I wanted to wish you a happy birthday," he told me.

"Uh, thanks, but my birthday was two days ago."

"I know and I feel real bad about that. So, to make it up to you I'm inviting you to dinner at my grandma's house. She'll make all my favorites—venison stew, wild rice, cranberry sauce, corn bread, fry bread, and chocolate cake for dessert. It will be a real feast."

"What? Your favorites? I thought it was my birthday celebration." I was trying not to laugh. I thought he'd forgotten. They'd even announced it over the loudspeaker at school last week. They always included birthdays for students and staff in the morning announcements. But he hadn't forgotten and now it was like someone was blowing little bubbles of happiness around me. Like someone was waving a wand but instead of blowing soap bubbles, they were bubbles of joy.

"It is but no reason we can't have all of my favorites."

"It does sound good, but are you sure your grandma won't mind?"

"It's fine, Cady. I'll meet you after school tomorrow and we can walk to her house together. I'll have my grandma call your dad and set it up. Got to run, got practice." Then he took off.

* * *

John Ray had told me to wait for him outside near the front doors. I always liked how welcoming the front of our school looks. Some of the kids had painted murals on big pieces of wood mounted on either side of the double doors. We'd had a visiting Ojibway artist come to our school and teach an art workshop for one week. He'd talked about how he used to drink a lot because he was afraid his art work would never be good enough.

"But then, one day, I decided to quit that negative thinking and give it a try. I picked up my paintbrush and never turned back," he told us. "It wasn't easy and it still isn't easy, but it was really worth it."

The kids in the workshop liked him because he told the truth. He said that art had given him a purpose in his life and helped him to overcome his addiction to alcohol and now he wanted to help others. My friend, Daryl, was one of the kids in his workshop and he explained to me how they made the murals.

First, they sketched the life-sized drawings on paper using pencils and then they drew designs on wooden panels. There were about eight kids in the workshop and they all helped paint the murals. Daryl told me that one of murals was his design. It showed an eagle soaring in the woods high above the pine trees. Sitting on the ground underneath it was a young man with his arms in the air looking up at the night sky. Through the tops of the trees you could see hundreds of tiny, bright gold stars. There was a small full moon in the upper left corner.

"We need that moon for balance, Cady. I'll let you figure out what that means," Daryl told me.

The other mural showed three women shawl dancers. The first time I looked at the mural, I felt as if I was actually dancing with the women shown in it. One woman wore a blue shawl with a white crane decorating its edge. Another wore a green shawl and at its bottom edge was shown a wolf howling at the moon. The last woman's shawl was red with a pattern in blue of bear claws along its bottom. I was with them dancing to the songs made by the beating drums. Each woman wore her hair long and braided and I loved looking at the detail of the beaded barrettes they wore in their hair. The dancer on the far right had one of her feet raised and I could see the beading on her moccasin. When I looked at that mural, I felt happy and proud of my heritage. These murals made our school special in a good way. They told the world who we were and that we were proud of our culture and our history.

"Caught you daydreaming?" John Ray laughed as he came through the front doors.

"No, I'm looking at the murals again. I love looking at them."

"Don't blame you, they're really something. Didn't your friend, Daryl, paint one of them?"

"Uh huh. He did a lot of the work. I think he's going to be an artist now."

And then we started walking down the road toward John Ray's grandma's house.

The sun was warm on our back; birds were singing from the trees lining both sides of the road. The gravel crunched under our feet and a woodpecker made that distinctive rat-a-tat-a-tat noise. His brightly colored red feathers moved as he attacked the top of an old tree. They like to drill dead trees and this one seemed either dead or dying. There is so much going on in nature if only people would open their eyes and ears to it.

A few minutes later, John Ray nudged my elbow.

"Cady, am I going too fast? Does your ankle still hurt?"

"No, it's fine. I'm almost completely healed now."

"That's good because there's something I want to show you."

We moved to the side of the road. John Ray crossed a drainage ditch and climbed up a small incline. He pushed aside some low hanging branches.

"Come on, Cady. It's up here."

I followed him and when I reached his side, he whispered, "Okay, now, no talking. Look where I'm pointing."

And, there, not more than five yards away from us was an albino fawn.

"There's a little spring back here and sometimes it shows up with its mom. I was hoping it would be here today so I could show it to you."

Then he bent down and kissed me ever so softly on my cheek.

"I've wanted to do that for a long time, Cady. Happy birthday."

His face was serious as he looked down at me, but then the corners of his mouth started to curve up into a smile. "We'd better go now. Come on."

I stood there stunned. Were my eyes filling with tears? Then I smiled, shook myself a little, and followed him.

CHAPTER 22
RIVER

~~~~~~~~

That kiss wasn't my only surprise that afternoon. Standing on the steps of Grandma Eunice's house was my Grandma Winnie!

"Cady, come here and give me a hug," she cried out. I ran into her arms and let her hold me. She hugged me tight to her chest and she was laughing. Soon I was laughing, too.

"But, Grandma, you didn't tell me you'd be here. Why didn't you tell me?" I was laughing and crying happy tears at the same time.

"Sure I did, Cady. I told you when you called that your uncle was bringing me here for an elders' meeting. I didn't give you my exact itinerary. Eunice and I thought it would be fun to surprise you and it looks like we have."

Grandma Eunice came out of the kitchen laughing and smiling as much as my grandma was.

"Now and then we older folks like to have our fun. And it looks like we pulled it off," she said, chuckling.

"You sure did, Grandma. When are we eating? I'm starving," John Ray said and rubbed his stomach.

"Oh, you, you're always hungry these days. Go get your grandpa out of the backyard and tell him dinner's ready and then you can wash up."

John Ray hadn't exaggerated. It was a feast. We had venison stew with wild rice, corn bread and fry bread. We had a salad with dried cranberries and walnuts and iced tea to drink. There was even a three-layer chocolate cake and ice cream for dessert.

"Let's clear the table of these dishes and then I think it's time for us to tell these young ones a story," Grandma Eunice declared.

"Yes. It's time Cady found out the story behind her necklace," my grandma added. She looked at me. "It's okay, Cady. It will be okay now."

I rooted around in my jeans pocket for a tissue to wipe my tears. I couldn't let myself cry because then I'd start making that awful snorting sound.

"Finally. This has been driving me crazy," I brushed a tear from my eye. And then I pressed my thumb into my other wrist, anything to hold the tears back.

"Don't cry, Cady. Tonight you will get your answers," Grandma said.

We moved into the living room. John Ray's grandparents sat down in matching brown leather recliners. John Ray settled in an overstuffed armchair covered in a soft green suede. My grandma settled on the flowered couch and patted the cushion next to her.

"Come here and sit down, Cady."

"Now that everyone is comfortable, I'll begin. The necklace once belonged to one of our elders." Her voice sounded so matter-of-fact. "Actually, it belonged to my great-grandmother," Grandma Eunice added. "It was handed down through the generations to the oldest girl in each family. Sometimes it brought them good luck and sometimes it didn't. It was a nice piece of jewelry, an adornment and sometimes magical things happened when the owner wore it, and sometimes they didn't."

"Until it went to Irene," Grandma whispered.

"Yes, until it went to Irene," Grandma Eunice repeated and then sighed.

John Ray and I glanced at each other. He shrugged his shoulders a little and looked away. I moved closer to my grandma. I wanted to hear more of the story.

"Go on, Winnie," Eunice added.

"Irene had grown up hearing the stories of the necklace, of course. Irene never believed much in those sorts of things, in special powers and magical happenings. She wanted to live in the moment. She wanted to have fun and enjoy life. Oh, she was something. And she really was a lot of fun."

"That she was," Grandma Eunice added. "She was a real firepot."

"And she loved to dance. Ever since she was a little girl she couldn't sit still.

"She'd jump and run and skip. She'd shuffle her feet and pretty soon she was dancing. We all noticed. She didn't even have to blurt out 'look at me, look at me' like so many of the little ones do nowadays. You couldn't help but watch her. She was so graceful. When she moved, she flowed," Grandma told us.

This is pretty interesting but what about the necklace?

"We're getting to that part, Cady." Grandma Winnie reached out to pat my hand.

Now I was wondering if she could read my mind because I hadn't said the words out loud. Both women smiled as if to say, *Kids today. So impatient. Not like in our day when we sat in the circle and listened.*

"Well, on with the story," Grandma Eunice continued. "The old folks noticed how much Irene liked to dance and how she was really good at it. They taught her all of our dances. She was just a little one and she'd be out there dancing to the beat of a hand drum. Now, these weren't sacred dances. She was too young for that. They were the dances of our people. Dances when we were happy, dances to celebrate a victory, dances to celebrate a bountiful harvest. There were dances to celebrate men coming back from a successful hunt. Oh, so many dances and that little Irene learned them all.

"We were so happy for her. She was so happy dancing that she made us happy to watch. We tried to keep up with her but we couldn't. She had the gift. Before she was 10 years old she was dancing with the grownups at the powwows and gatherings. She was such a pretty little thing and she attracted a lot of attention. We were all very protective of her. Of course, we were little ones ourselves and didn't really know we were protecting her but we wanted her to be happy and to keep dancing. We'd help her with anything she needed so she could keep dancing."

Both grandmas were so lost in the story that they seemed like young girls again. Even their voices sounded younger. For a few precious minutes, they sounded like young girls chattering in the lunchroom at school.

"Well, Eunice, you know how it was," Grandma commented.

"Yes, well, I suppose we hoped that maybe some of her specialness would rub off on us. She really was something. Now keep going, Winnie."

"Well, Irene had her first moon time on her 12th birthday. That's a very special time for a woman and her family wanted to honor it in some way. That's when they decided to give her the necklace that you found. And, of course, she loved it. She wore it every day for almost a year until her parents told her she would wear it out. Her father made her that little leather pouch to wear around her neck and she placed the necklace inside of it. As far as I know, Irene never went anywhere without that necklace.

"Things went on like that for the next few years. I've already told you about when we were young girls together. I've thought about those years so often but I've never talked about them until you visited me a few weeks ago."

"Yes, Winnie, it's been the same with me," Grandma Eunice said, her voice sounding almost wistful.

"When you visited me, Cady, it was so good to see you and so good to speak of these things," my grandma said. But I didn't tell you the whole story. After Irene moved to this town, the one where you are living now, she fell in love. I told you that. And I told you how Irene and her husband fell in love and how they'd go out dancing. Such innocent fun. Two beautiful young people going out after a long week of work to let off some steam.

"Neither one of them ever touched a drop of alcohol. They'd seen too many of their relatives hurt by drinking and didn't want to bring it into their lives. But that doesn't mean that others didn't drink. One night, they were walking home from a local dance when an old man lost control of his car and ran into the two of them. He drove off but the police later caught him and later he spent several years in jail for leaving the scene of an accident.

"Irene's man was killed. He didn't die right away though. No, his spirit died first. Bad luck for such a good man. They had to amputate his left leg above the knee. He was okay for a few months. He seemed to be okay and joked about having a peg leg. But he was never the same. There was a sadness to him that hadn't been there before. Of course, he couldn't dance anymore. Eventually, he was so sad that he tried to end his relationship with Irene."

"Oh, no, Grandma, that's so sad."

"Yes, Cady, it was. She told me he kept asking her these same two questions. *Who will hire me? How will I support us?*

"And although he never talked about it, we knew it was slowly killing him that he couldn't dance. He couldn't hold Irene in his arms and move her across the floor. The two of them had been so graceful and happy as if they'd been made for dancing and for the rest of the world to watch them.

"But after the accident, there would be no more town dances, no more powwow dances for him, no more ceremonial dances for that proud young man. As brave as he was, we all knew he was suffering. And Irene was suffering along with him. That's why she announced one day that she would never dance again. And that's your story, Cady." Grandma Winnie reached over to pat my hand.

"Why wasn't that in the story I read in the newspaper?" I wanted to know. "I'll show you the notes I made about the newspaper story I found at the library. I've got them over there in my backpack." I rose out of my chair and reached for my backpack.

"Oh, Cady, I don't need to read your notes or even see the story. I lived through it. I'm sure it's the one you're talking about," my grandma said. A tear rolled down her cheek. She glanced away and brushed her sleeve across her face.

"But that's not the end of it. Is it, Winnie?" John Ray's grandma asked.

"No, it's not. Hold my hand, Cady, while I tell you the rest." She touched my cheek with her finger. "You see, Cady, sometimes life can be so very, very sad. Irene's man died later that year. He was walking across that bridge on the north side of town. He was pretty good at walking with a wooden leg and his crutches, but it was icy one night and he fell into the river. Irene was with him and the best we can figure is that she jumped in after him to try to save him. She always was the best swimmer in our group. But he was a big man, much bigger than Irene and the current is so strong in the river. They might have survived but an awful storm had come up that night and, well, they were gone."

John Ray's grandma sat with her hands in her lap. Like my grandma, she had to wipe a tear off her face. And then, as if using one voice, the two women said, "I'm glad we've told them."

"So, now you know. And that's the story of two of the best people we've ever known," Grandma Winnie ended.

"And who were taken from us too young," Grandma Eunice added.

I sat there too stunned to move. It was a lot to take in and now I knew why John Ray's grandma had been so upset when I found the photo the day I had interviewed her. Now I knew that my grandma and his grandma had grown up together and been friends together as little girls and were still friends.

"Thank you, both of you, for telling me this story. I never knew there was so much history behind the necklace." I looked around the room. I felt sadness for those who had died too young. But I was also relieved that I now knew the story behind the necklace but I was still confused.

"*Megwetch* for telling me the story but I still don't know why I found the necklace. Am I supposed to do something special with it?"

"Yes, Cady, but it's not all sad history. That necklace has blessed you. It found you for a reason and I think that very soon you will know what that reason is," Grandma Eunice emphasized.

"It found you for a reason, dear girl," my grandma added. "And now you must wait patiently to find out what that reason is. It will come to you."

"Will the reason come in my dreams? I'm not very patient and I hope it comes soon."

But neither of our grandmas answered me. A few minutes later, truck tires crunched over gravel driveway outside.

"Cady, that's it for tonight. I recognize your dad's truck out there." Grandma Eunice stood at the front window and had pulled aside the curtains to gaze outside.

There was a knock on the door. Dad was standing on the porch. I could see him through the screen door. He wore a pair of brown corduroy pants, a long-sleeved and crisply ironed black shirt and black tasseled slip-on shoes. He had dressed up for the elders because he usually wore an old pair of boots. He even wore black dress socks. His long hair was pulled off his face in a loose ponytail that trailed down his back but he'd tied it off in three- to four-inch sections. His face was freshly shaven and the scent of his favorite cologne filled the air.

"Well, son, some things don't change. You still dress up for the ladies," my grandma said laughing. A broad smile filled her face.

"Yes, Mom, and you and Miss Eunice are my favorite ladies. This is like old times."

He crossed the room in a few graceful strides. And then he and my grandma hugged like they hadn't seen each other in ages instead of since our last visit.

"It sure is," Grandma Eunice said. "And it's about time we all got back together. Can you stay a bit and drink some coffee? I've brewed a fresh pot and I think I've got a bit of dessert left. What do you say?"

"For you and your cake, any time."

Who was this man? Dad is dressed up and happy to be visiting with the old folks. He's like the dad I remember from when I was a little girl. Maybe things really are changing. Maybe my life is actually improving.

But I didn't have long to think about this. There was a tapping at the window. That pesky blue jay perched on the outside windowsill. He was hitting his beak repeatedly into the glass.

"Someone wants your attention, Cady. Better go out and see to it," Grandma told me.

I left the grownups to their visiting and coffee drinking and stepped out the front door. I tried not to let the door slam too loudly because I didn't want to startle the bird but he flew away. Something told me to follow him. I stepped off the porch and took a dirt path that cut across a patch of grass to a shed. It was big enough to hold a lawn mower, a snow blower and some bikes. Someone must have painted it green recently because it still had that fresh-paint smell. It was there I found John Ray. He'd been looking at something on the ground and looked up at me once I was standing near him.

"Did you solve your mystery tonight now that you know the story behind your necklace?"

"Sort of. I found out where the necklace came from and who its last owner was. I still don't know why I was the one to find it, but I'm happy that my grandma and your grandma told me the story. It all seems so real. Even though the Irene they told me about died a long time ago it feels as if I know her somehow. When I hold that necklace, it's like she's with me. Do you think that's strange?"

"No. Do you think it's strange that our grandmas have known each other since they were kids?" John Ray asked me in return.

"Not really. I think it's nice and it explains to me why your grandma let me interview her. I think she wanted to do something good for my grandma," I replied.

"Good thing we're not from the same clan."

I started blushing because even though he'd only kissed me once, I knew he liked me. And we both knew getting closer would be impossible if we were from the same clan.

"I wanted to talk to you away from the others and tell you something. I'll be leaving here soon for the summer. I've got some relatives in North Dakota my grandpa wants me to visit. They're going to put me out to fast the old-time way. I'll study with the elders and learn some of their ceremonies.

He stared at the ground after he'd told me this and watched a small turtle make its leisurely way across the tall grass. A small tear started in the corner of my left eye. I turned away because I didn't want him to see me cry.

He added, "I'll miss you. I don't think I'll have much time to myself and I'm not sure where I'll be staying so don't be surprised if you don't hear from me. But I'll be thinking of you."

"And me. I'll be thinking of you," I whispered. I repeated it again, a bit louder this time, to make sure he had heard me.

Soon we would be separated by distance and I hoped our connection would stay strong. Time away from each other might even make this connection grow stronger. Looking deeper into my culture had brought many blessings. I had the honor of interviewing Grandma Eunice. I found the necklace and wanting to learn its story had brought me closer my family. And now my dad was back visiting his long-time friends on the reservation.

"Will you miss me, Cady?"

"Of course."

My hands were in the front pocket of my hoodie where I liked to put them when I was nervous and my fingers were busy rubbing my lucky stone. It was an ordinary stone but it was heart-shaped and almost a pale pink in color.

"Here." I handed him the stone. "Carry this with you. It's brought me luck and now it's your turn. It's from the first night we met at the beach."

"*Megwetch*, Cady." His hand reached for the stone. He held my hand and then reached out for me. He wrapped his arms around me and he kissed me ever so softly.

This time it was A real kiss, a kiss on the lips, and not on my cheek. And from a boy I really like. I had closed my eyes during the kiss and now I opened them. I looked into John Ray's eyes and they had a teasing look to them. His mouth was curved into a broad smile. I smiled back at him.

It was a nice way to thank me.

Chapter 23
East/When the Sun Comes Up

School ended for the year. I had survived eighth grade at a new school and would be a freshman in the fall. My step-mother went back to her part-time job at the donut shop the second week in June. She said she would need me to babysit for my little brother.

"Tips are pretty good there, Cady, and this time I'll pay you with real money and not leftover donuts. It's only for the summer to fill in while the others take their vacations. You're good with the baby and he really loves you and this way your dad is not tied down all the time."

I agreed and was already shopping online for some new running gear and some new clothes. I'd grown another inch and my clothes didn't fit very well anymore. My brother in Minneapolis wanted me to visit again and we planned to drive to my grandma's to spend a weekend with her. And, best of all, there would be a special one-week volleyball camp at school in July and Dad would watch my baby brother that week so I could attend.

"Sports are important, Cady. I can see how much running has done for you and I know you'll get a lot out of this camp. The fees aren't too bad and I want you to go. I played sports as a kid and was darned good at it," he told me.

Lately, it felt like it used to between us and that made me happy. And then I had a strange thought.

Running has helped me. And finding the necklace had brought me closer to my family. Moving here and transferring to an Indian school has brought me closer to my culture and to to my heritage. I've met John Ray and he introduced me to his grandmother. I'd even learned to do beadwork!

"Cady, are you listening to me?" Dad was holding a big wooden spoon in his hand and waving it around.

I jumped a little because he'd startled me out of my thoughts.

"What? Oh, this." He held up the big spoon. "I'm cooking some pudding on the stove and need this to move it around. Did you even hear a word I said?"

"Um, not really."

"The other night when I picked you up when you were visiting your grandmother, I received a pretty tempting offer. It seems the elders have put together a plan to run a language immersion camp this summer. They're worried that our language is being lost because not enough of the young people are learning it and speaking it. There is so much contained within our language. It's more than words. It's our culture, our traditions, our belief systems and our spirituality."

I nodded. I had listened to him say this many times when talking to his friends and to Bruce. But he'd never talked to me about it in this way. Now he was talking to me as if I were an adult and not a kid.

"They've asked me to oversee the program. It will be a one-week class and your grandma and John Ray's grandma are going to teach also. Your brother will come down for it and I want you to attend too. It's time you learned our language and this will be a good start."

I don't think he noticed the happy expression on my face because he'd moved back to the stove and was now stirring the pudding.

"I hope chocolate's okay. I know butterscotch is your favorite but I was in a chocolate sort of mood today."

He started humming one of those old-time country western songs he liked so much.

"Chocolate's fine, Dad."

I climbed the stairs up to my bedroom. I wanted to write about this amazing day in my journal and then I planned to call Irish.

My life wasn't perfect but it was getting better. I was actually looking forward to summer even if John Ray would be living in a different state. We liked each other and that was enough to make me happy. He would come home when he finished his training. I wondered if he'd change. I was about to call Irish (we have a landline phone with an extension upstairs) when my stepmother knocked on my door.

"Lights out, Cady, it's past eleven o'clock. If your brother wasn't teething and acting so fussy, I'd have been asleep by now. Lights out and no phoning Irish."

Her footsteps sounded lightly on the wooden floor as she crossed the hall into her own bedroom. There was that reassuring creak the floor made when she walked over the worn spots.

"Your dad will be checking, Cady, so go to sleep," she finished and shut the door to her bedroom.

It was late and I knew I'd see Irish tomorrow at the mall. She'd planned another shopping excursion. Her newest boyfriend was taking her to a movie this weekend and she wanted to shop for a new outfit.

"I need some things, Cady, and I want you to come with me. Meet me in front of the fountain at the mall. I can get there by 4 o'clock."

Irish always made me laugh and I was looking forward to it.

I switched off the small lamp next to my bed and snuggled down into my quilt. I was tired but restless. I turned over and then turned over again. I flipped my pillow over to the cool side and nestled into its softness. I fell asleep reliving that moment when John Ray's lips touched mine. His lips were so soft. Who knew a boy's lips could be that soft? I remembered the look in his eyes and how good his hand felt on my shoulder. All of it was so delicious. I fell asleep hoping I'd have dreams as happy as this memory.

It was dark when I was startled awake by tapping against my window. I propped myself up on my elbow and shook my head.

What had I been dreaming? Who was that woman I'd seen in my dreams? And then I remembered. It was the woman in the photograph. It was my grandma's friend, Irene, and she was glowing. In my dream she held the necklace in her hand and motioned me with her other hand to come closer. I walked up to her as she held the necklace out to me.

"Take it now, little one. It is yours. May its magic help you, but always remember to treat it with honor."

I stood there stunned and wanted to ask her questions. I moved my mouth but nothing came out. I was so frustrated I wanted to cry.

"But, but," was all I managed to say before I woke fully. I got up to use the bathroom. The baby was fussing and crying again. Then I overheard Dad say, "It's okay, Francine. I'll take care of him. Go back to sleep."

Then Dad started to sing Colson the same simple lullaby about a baby rocking in a tree that he used to sing to me. Dad glanced up and saw me standing in the doorway.

Maybe it was the woman in the dream, maybe it was hearing the lullaby, or maybe it was making new friends and solving the mystery of the necklace. Maybe it was all of those things that was making me happy.

Walking to the window, my eyes adjusted to the dark and it was a full moon. There on my windowsill was that silly blue jay. It pecked at the window with its beak, then twitched its head.

That silly bird seemed to wink at me and then it flew off. Or did it? Did I really see it or imagine it? What was happening?

The flashlight was where I kept it next to my bed. Grabbing it I walked to my closet and pulled up the loose floorboard. I took the leather pouch and went back into my bedroom. I balanced the flashlight on the table and opened the pouch. I had to see that necklace again. I put it around my neck and as I did I remembered something my culture teacher had taught us.

"Our world, the Indian world, is circular. We're not a linear culture like the West. Think of a big tree. Imagine a limb is missing from that tree. Where that limb once was you now see a circle with rings starting in the middle and circling around and around to the outer edges. That's how I want you to think."

So much had happened in the month since I'd found the necklace and one thing had led to another and then another, just like those tree rings my teacher Iris had taught us about. John Ray had helped me. Grandma Eunice, Grandma Winnie, Bruce and even Francine had helped. I'd found out more than the story of the necklace. I learned a piece of our family's history. I found out that people could be kind and would help me if I asked. I found out that I was stronger than I thought. And now I wanted to stay in that circle.

I turned off the flashlight and fell asleep with the necklace around my neck.

* * *

Irish was waiting for me at the mall's fountain the next day.

"Here, I brought you an end-of-the-year present," she said and handed me a cold can of my favorite ginger ale. I popped the soda open and gulped it down.

"*Megwetch.*"

"Dork." Then she punched my arm.

"Right back at you," I said but I was laughing so hard I snorted the soda.

We went inside and while she tried on clothes I thought about all that had happened since I'd found the necklace. Just a few weeks ago, all I could think about was running away or going to live somewhere else but now I wanted to stay here with my friends. The beautiful woman in my dream last night told me to wear the necklace with pride and to honor my heritage.

"The strength lies in you and not in the necklace. Sometimes you have to trust others and sometimes you have to trust yourself and sometimes you have to listen to a crazy blue jay when he gives you advice. He's yours now and he'll be back," she had whispered.

I had my answer. We believe that answers are not always given in straightforward words. The woman in my dream had told me to look to myself for the woman I am to become. She had told me to listen to the teachings of my elders and to pay attention to their words. Best of all, she had told me to trust myself.

That night I went to my room around 10 o'clock. I left the room's window shade up so that I could gaze at the full moon from my bed. A few minutes later, I saw that silly blue jay perched on the window sill. It winked at me and then flew off.

"Until next time, you crazy blue jay." I turned over and went to sleep because I knew there would be a next time. The woman in my dream had told me so.

Acknowledgments

I wrote the first draft (which was followed by many more) of *Cady* years ago after promising my students that I would write a book for them. I believe we teach by example and hope to inspire them to use their own words to tell their stories. There are so many I wish to thank for their help along the way. They include, but are not limited to:

- The University of Wisconsin-Madison Department of Continuing Studies

- Haley Greenfeather English for her wonderful cover showing Cady brought to life.

- The young readers from Stephenson (MI) Elementary School for their suggestions.

- For Gina and Linda for the many hours they spent reading draft after draft...and for their encouragement.

- To Kira Henschel, an incredibly supportive publisher.

- To the Highlights Foundation workshops, Wild Acres Retreat Center and Split Rock Arts summer workshop/ University of Minnesota for continuing instruction and support.

- To my many friends and the wonderful libraries of Marinette, WI and Menominee, MI.

- And to my two sons, daughter-in-law, granddaughter, and mother who believe in the power of storytelling.

Discussion Questions for Cady and the Bear Necklace

1. Which one of the characters are you most like?

2. Draw a Venn Diagram to compare and contrast your answer to question number 1.

3. Give a brief summary of the story including four or five important details.

4. What was the main lesson of this story?

5. Name parts of the book which helped you to predict what would happen next.

6. Cady wanted to learn the story of the necklace. How did she investigate its history?

7. Have you ever found something and wondered about its past? Explain.

8. Cady and Irish have different personalities. What are three adjectives to describe Cady and three adjectives to describe Irish?

9. What advice would you give Cady about moving somewhere new? About making new friends? About learning to live with a new stepmom?

10. Cady said she had trouble controlling her temper. Did she learn to control it by the end of the story? How do you know?

11. Do you know someone who reminds you of Cady?

12. What did you learn from reading this book that you didn't know before?

13. What did the cover make you think about?

14. How important will Cady's journal be in her next adventure?

15. What do you think will be Cady's next adventure?

ABOUT THE AUTHOR

Ann Dallman has won numerous awards for her writing and has presented her work at national conferences. She graduated from the University of Wisconsin-Madison (Journalism Education) and received her MA from Viterbo University.

A former teacher, she has written for *Marquette Monthly, Country, Farm and Ranch, Winds of Change, Chess Life, Salon Today,* and *American Salon* magazines, and the *Green Bay Press Gazette*. She was the writer and organizing force behind the book *Sam English: The Life, Times and Works of an Artist,* 2009 PEAK International Award winner, and compiled/edited *The Hannahville Poets.*

She resides in Menominee, Michigan.

Contact information:
The author: lakemichiganpen@gmail.com
The cover artist: www.Haleygreenfeatherart.com

CPSIA information can be obtained
at www.ICGtesting.com
Printed in the USA
FSHW020617070819
60757FS